MW00904434

THREE TIMES CHARMED

Teas & Temptations Mysteries
Book Three

CINDY STARK

www.cindystark.com

Three Times Charmed © 2018 C. Nielsen

Cover Design by Kelli Ann Morgan
Inspire Creative Services

License Notes

Welcome to Stonebridge, Massachusetts

Welcome to Stonebridge, a small town in Massachusetts where the label "witch" is just as dangerous now as it was in 1692. From a distance, most would say the folks in Stonebridge are about the friendliest around. But a dark and disturbing history is the backbone that continues to haunt citizens of this quaint town where many have secrets they never intend to reveal.

Visit www.cindystark.com for more titles and release information. Sign up for Cindy's newsletter to ensure you're always hearing the latest happenings.

PROLOGUE

Stonebridge, Massachusetts 1689

With the sun hovering low on the horizon. Clarabelle's mother climbed down from their wagon and joined Clarabelle and her father on the ground. She focused a stern gaze on Clarabelle. "Remember, head up. No emotion."

She swallowed and nodded. "Yes, Mama."

On the most horrific day of her life, her mother wanted her to act like she didn't care. Like it didn't matter that her best friend since she was four wouldn't live to see her eighteenth birthday. Like Genevieve and her mother deserved to be punished for their blood and their religion.

Like her very heart wouldn't die with them.

Those two women in contrast valued all life and had never hurt a soul.

Blessed Mother help them all.

Her mother grabbed her, her fingers curling tight around Clarabelle's hand. They followed Clarabelle's father and other solemn townsfolk along the dirt trail that led to Redemption Pond.

Clarabelle wanted to scream at the insane people in town, to run and hide. But if she didn't show her face and support the laws of

Stonebridge, she would likely be next. Especially since people knew she and Genevieve were friends.

Part of her wanted to die with Genevieve.

The other half wanted to live for revenge, to make those who caused this terrible suffering scream in pain. She'd promised Genevieve this much.

Families had gathered around the edge of the pond. A small boat staked to the shore floated on the calm, mirror-like surface. A large pile of ominous stones rested next to the stake.

Her throat clenched. Hot tears filled her eyes, and she glanced downward, lest someone notice. *Oh, Blessed Mother.* Those rocks would ensure Genevieve could not take another breath once she was pushed into the water.

"Head up," her mother whispered harshly.

Clarabelle bit hard on her tongue until she tasted blood, hoping the pain would stave off the tears until they'd left this public display of insanity. She blinked quickly and lifted her head.

Thankfully, her father chose a spot toward the back of the crowd to stop, and she liked to believe he'd done this as a merciful gesture to her.

Electric tension charged the air, and the crowd grew silent. The distant, muffled cries of two women floated on the silent breeze. Clarabelle bit her tongue harder. The taste of metal coated her tongue. If she knew any blood spells to curse these putrid people, she'd mutter one right now.

The sobs grew closer. She hated herself for not glancing toward Genevieve one last time, but after Mary Brown had been tried and convicted only a week ago, they'd all promised to deny friendship if one of them was caught.

Powerful anguish from the two women ripped through the air, slicing deep into Clarabelle's soul. She worked to shield herself from the piercing agony and failed. She and Genevieve had been friends for too long, their tapestries shared too many threads, and Clarabelle knew she would ache from this loss for the rest of her life.

The worst was Genevieve was innocent of the act for which she'd been accused. Their chickens had laid more eggs than other families in two weeks. In a jealous fit, one of the women in town had accused her and her mother of casting magic upon their chickens.

Those with power in town had agreed, and none dared argue. When they'd shaved Genevieve and her mother's heads, they'd discovered birthmarks, known signs of the Devil.

"I'll give you one last chance to beg for mercy from God," a man's voice boomed. The muffled cries grew to outright screams, and Clarabelle was certain they'd removed the gags from their mouths.

"Cursed be the day you were born," Genevieve's mother screamed. She followed with a string of words Clarabelle couldn't understand, but she was certain they must be curses. Then she suddenly stopped, and Genevieve's crying grew louder.

The horrific sounds slashed into her heart like razors, and she closed her eyes again, trying to block out the world.

"Please don't kill us," Genevieve begged between sobs. "We've done nothing wrong. We've hurt no one. *Please.*"

"Are you asking the almighty Lord for forgiveness?" the man asked.

"I–I've done nothing to need forgiveness. Please, please, you must listen."

"Gag her," called someone from the crowd, and Genevieve screamed again. She was immediately silenced.

Sounds of scuffling and increased muffled cries punched Clarabelle's stomach, and she was sure they were loading the victims into the boat. Although Clarabelle had barely eaten that day, she feared she'd vomit anyway.

Her mother's hand tightened around hers, and she forced herself to breathe.

Soft sobs came from somewhere in the crowd, and Clarabelle prayed they didn't belong to Eliza or Lily. She'd seen neither of them since Genevieve's arrest and had no idea how they fared.

Cries from the boat faded as the rower put distance between them and the shore. Clarabelle silently said a prayer that all of them could be strong and face whatever was coming. That Genevieve would find peace regardless of how she passed.

"Margaret Addison and Genevieve Addison, you have been convicted by a court of law." John Henry Parrish's words boomed over the water, and Clarabelle cursed his strong voice.

"You have been sentenced to death by drowning. May the Devil take your soul, and may the Father protect the god-fearing people upon this earth."

Raging fear soaked the atmosphere. Clarabelle focused on the brown, woolen cloak worn by the woman in front of her and tried to push all emotion away.

A splash echoed across the distance, and she gasped.

Her mother dug sharp fingernails into her flesh.

Clarabelle's face grew hot, and she couldn't breathe. She leaned against her mother for support.

Another splash.

She tried to swallow, but her mouth was drier than old cotton.

The voices of those around her rose, and people turned away. The show they'd come to see was over.

But for her, it wasn't.

Sensations of struggling for breath overwhelmed her, tightening her chest and leaving her lightheaded. Fear and anger collided.

Cold. And darkness. So much darkness.

Clarabelle fought to send love and light in the direction of Genevieve and her mother. *Please be okay. Please.*

Then peace. No more fear. No more pain. Only peace.

Clarabelle could breathe again.

When she did, fiery rage filled her lungs along with oxygen. They had stolen something precious from her, and they would pay.

With blood.

CHAPTER ONE

Current Day

Hazel Hardy entered her living room after a long day at work, teacup in hand, and found a fat orange tabby crouched on her reading chair, watching her with that sassy expression he always used.

The cat, with his odd, mysterious ways, had lived with her long enough to know that after work and dinner, she'd head for her favorite spot to read and relax. He'd proven to her time and again that he had an intelligence beyond most felines, and for that very reason she knew he lounged in her space on purpose.

She strode forward with a stern expression, hoping to intimidate him. She was the boss in this house, and he needed to learn that. "Get out of my chair."

He yawned and regarded her with a bored expression.

She set her cup on the table next to the chair and reached out with both hands, prepared to pick him up and physically remove him from her spot. The moment her fingers were an inch away from his soft fur, he sprang up and ran for the cover of the couch.

She narrowed her gaze. "One of these days you're going to give me a heart attack, and then there will be no one to take care of you." Though, from the looks of him, he'd managed to eat well before he'd begun to stalk her.

Hazel turned to claim her spot, but her ancestral grandmother's ancient book of spells now sat where the cat had been. That little stinker. He'd seemingly managed to open her underwear drawer, dig beneath all her panties and bras, and pull out her grandmother's tome.

Apparently thinking that drawer might be the safest place in the house to hide one of her darkest secrets had been a mistake on her part. She could question how he'd managed such a feat, but that went along with wondering how he'd escaped her house when all the windows and doors had been closed and locked.

Where Mr. Kitty was concerned she'd learned not to question anything.

That didn't mean she would take his sass without giving some back.

She lifted the book and then shot the cat, *her cat,* she supposed, a narrow-eyed glare. "Why is this here?"

The orange tabby stared at her as though he regarded an imbecile.

His attitude did nothing to ingratiate him to her. "Don't you know it's not polite for a man to rifle through a lady's lingerie drawer?"

If she didn't know better, she'd swear he lifted a sardonic brow.

She kept her gaze on him as she moved the spell book to the table next to her chair. She sat and picked up the thriller she'd been reading, instead.

She showed him the cover and smirked. "I don't know why you think you get to tell me what to do in my own house. You're the guest here. I'm the one who goes to work to make the money that buys your food, so you can stay fat and sassy."

He let out a long caterwaul followed by several short bursts of meowing that sounded an awful lot like he was telling her off. When he was finished, he shifted a suggestive gaze to the spell book on the table.

She flicked a glance at it and then looked back to him. "No."

Yes. You must.

Of course, he'd pull the creepy mind communication when he didn't get his way. She had so many reasons to boot his orange butt out the door, but this was why she kept him. He knew things she didn't. Things she feared she'd need to know if she intended to stay in the town that had stolen her heart.

Must? Why must she read it? She'd certainly been curious enough when she'd first found it, but the darker than dark spells at the back of the book had left her...uncomfortable.

Her mother had pounded the message to stay away from black magic into her brain so often during her childhood that she'd become annoyed. *We are not the type of witches who tap into that power. To do so is to invite things into your life that you don't want.*

Like she would ever consider messing with danger. She'd lived her whole life using her magic to help and heal people. It wasn't in her to do otherwise.

But she'd also never had it thrust right into her face like this, either. And the whole "must" thing stirred the worry inside her. Stonebridge might look quaint on the outside, but she'd discovered it also had a shadow side, which left her anxious.

She looked back to Mr. Kitty who still watched her with a serious yet annoyed expression. "I've already looked at this. I've learned everything I need to know."

Look again. You need to learn.

"There's nothing in there that will help me with my life. I know all about brews and potions, and I use those in my teas to make people less stressed, fall in love, and feel better. My life is happy the way it is. I don't need to learn anything else."

You need to protect yourself.

His understated warning sent chills skittering across her skin, but she still couldn't honor his request. "No, I don't. I know the rules and the cautions of living in Stonebridge. Cora gave me a concealing spell if I ever need to use magic. Which I don't intend to do."

She wanted Mr. Kitty to help guide her, but not when it came to dark magic.

She pointedly opened to where she had left off reading the thriller and did her best to ignore the intense energy that blasted from Mr. Kitty's direction. She wouldn't be controlled by a cat. A crazy one at that.

She was in charge of her destiny. "Maybe someday I will want to go back through it, but not now. Today, I want peace and to lose myself in a world of murder and mystery. So, bug off."

If you don't learn, you'll have no peace. Dead or alive, you will find no peace.

Again, his ominous warning stirred the anxiety inside her until it boiled. She growled her frustration at him.

Mr. Kitty crawled from beneath the couch, not threatened at all by her outburst, and jumped onto the coffee table in front of Hazel where he proceeded to look her directly in the eye. *Don't make me tell your grandmother.*

Son of a crunchy biscuit. The last time she was at Clarabelle's house, she'd had something of a conversation with her ancient grandmother's ghost. Hazel had innocently managed to trigger unfounded fears for her grandmother. The last thing she wanted to do was upset her further.

If she didn't appear to try to learn, Mr. Kitty would make sure she couldn't visit her grandmother again without repercussions.

Not only that, Hazel intended to purchase Clarabelle's house, and she'd hoped to make a good life there. For that, she needed a happy grandma ghost.

Hazel sighed and shot a disgusted look at her cat. "Fine," she said in a snarky voice. "I will read it tonight, but tomorrow, we're back to the thriller. Understand?"

Her cat watched her until she picked up the book of spells and opened it. Then he jumped off the table, crawled back under the couch, and curled himself into a ball where he would likely fall asleep.

She opened the cover to the front page and caught sight of Clarabelle's quote again. *Better to follow your heart, or you're already dead.*

Had her grandmother meant that about life in general, to a man, or to following the prompting of her heart where spells were concerned? She wished she knew that and so much more.

Except not about her dark spells.

Hazel hesitated, wondering if Mr. Kitty would hear her switch the books again and then decided he'd know if she did. Instead, she flipped to the page she'd marked with a kiddie bookmark she'd obtained from the library.

The Wrath of the Damned.

CHAPTER TWO

The title of the spell gave Hazel shivers. "The Wrath of the Damned," she whispered. Sounded horribly ominous to her. She supposed that was the point.

This would be the spell that her grandmother had used to create what the residents called the infamous Witches' Wrath. The nor'easter storm Clarabelle and her cohorts had created ravaged Stonebridge every year around Ostara as punishment for the town who'd persecuted the them for their beliefs.

On the next page, she found instructions for evaporating water.

A hair from each of the witches.

Blessed water from Redemption Pond. The place where the pious townsfolk had laden Clarabelle's pockets with stones before they'd ruthlessly pushed her and her friends overboard and left them to drown. Her grandmother must have known what was in store and had given survival her best shot.

She wondered if they had tried the spell out in advance, or if the moment they'd sunk to the bottom, they'd had no idea whether their attempt would work.

And worse, what it must have been like to realize they'd failed. The thought left her sad.

Blood of the accuser.

Three simple ingredients. Still, she couldn't help but wonder how they'd thought they could manage to collect blood from their accusers.

She wished there was an easier way to learn more about her ancestor's history. Maybe Hazel needed to reconsider fully reading the book. Maybe then, she'd find clues as to what had happened during those last few days before Stonebridge's citizens had tried and convicted her.

During Hazel's first attempt to read the entire book, she'd smiled at the childlike scrawling that detailed how to find edible mushrooms or how to calm a cow before milking. Those spells included who'd taught them and, frequently, the name was Mama.

As she'd turned the pages, the writing had grown smoother with a distinctive flair that Hazel supposed had been common during that time. Those spells had come from many different sources besides Clarabelle's mother.

Eventually, Clarabelle had become the creator of spells, including the darkest ones that appeared last in the book. If Hazel understood Mr. Kitty correctly, she was expected to learn everything inside, even if she knew she'd never use it.

Not knowing where to start reading this time, she closed her eyes and ran a finger over the edge of the pages waiting for a spark of knowing from the universe. When it came, she slid her fingernail into the space and opened to that page. As she read the words, she drew her brows into a curious and uncertain frown.

From what she could tell, this was a spell for money.

Huh? That didn't seem horribly awful. Like could this make her rich?

The idea appealed to her. If she had to learn something new, this didn't seem so bad. And money, if used correctly, could provide lots of positive outcomes.

A coin as an offering.

Blood from the seeker.

She blocked out her mother's words that warned of anything requiring blood. Blood spells were dark spells regardless of how innocent they might seem.

Then again, her mother had no idea what it was like to be caught between two worlds like she was. Her mom *had* told her to be careful and protect herself. Practicing this spell would likely fall under that category since she knew Mr. Kitty would make her life miserable if she didn't do something.

Burn over the flame of desire until the two become one.

That's it? She could place a drop of her blood on a penny and heat it with fire, and then the universe would grant her more money?

She shut the book with a snap. Mr. Kitty startled and sent her a nasty glare.

Holy harpies. She was so doing that right now. She could be rich by tomorrow. Then she could buy Clarabelle's house and anything else she wanted. How cool would that be?

Just because her mother had only taught her passive spells didn't make all the others wrong. Hazel had a heritage of rich blood in her veins, and it would be a shame not to explore it a little.

She assembled the ingredients in her kitchen. A penny. A pin to prick her finger. A lighter and a pair of pliers to hold the penny while she burned it. This was much simpler than the spell she'd tried to grow her lashes longer. There was no way she could get this one wrong.

Before she began the spell, she whispered the words Cora had taught her so that she could conceal any trace of her magic from the world.

"Close their eyes. Cover their ears. Let me practice with no fears. When in this space, no one shall see...the magic that I bring to be. I deem this true, so mote it be."

Then came time for the pin prick. She wasn't one who could easily inflict pain on herself, but one small bit of discomfort would be worth the outcome, right? Even if this spell was blood magic, she wasn't cursing anyone or asking for unearthly power.

Which is what Clarabelle must have done to drain the lake. The thought bewildered her.

Enough procrastination. She placed the pin over her finger and inhaled. With a quick stab, the tip pierced her skin, and she grimaced from the prick of pain. She dropped the pin and squeezed the tip of her finger until the blood welled into a red bud.

Her heart thumped loudly as she turned her finger downward and continued squeezing until a drop fell onto the penny. She carefully secured the penny between the tips of the pliers and then flicked on the lighter. It took a few moments for the penny to heat, but when it did, blood bubbled on the surface.

She cast a quick glance at the tome and carefully repeated the words scrawled on the page.

"A sacrifice is made as my thanks to thee. A willing gift of blood in exchange for money. This wish will be granted, so mote it be."

When the blood became dried rust on the penny, she released the lighter and dropped it on the kitchen counter. The hot penny glowed with energy as she set it on a ceramic plate, and then she paused to study her work.

She didn't feel different, didn't feel richer, and she wondered how long it would take before her spell went into effect. It wasn't as if her phone was ringing with someone on the other end giving her the news that she had inherited a million dollars from a long-lost aunt.

Maybe it was one of those spells that took time. That was fine with her. She had all the time in the world.

Or maybe she'd done it wrong. Or maybe her innocent heart wouldn't allow her to illicit such magic. Either way, she could say she'd tried to learn.

She turned and startled. Kitty was perched on the table, watching with approval in his eyes.

"Why do you have to do that? Can't you be a normal kitty who doesn't maim and scare the daylights out of his owner?"

He chuffed, jumped to the floor, and strode away with his tail high in the air as if to say no one owned him.

She shook her head in annoyance.

By the time she put away her tools, the penny had cooled. She gently picked it up and carried it upstairs with her into her bedroom where she placed it under her pillow. This way, it would be out of sight.

Not that anyone would be in her house to find it. But she'd messed with magic, something she'd promised her mother she wouldn't do once she was in Stonebridge. After what had happened to poor Clarabelle, she wasn't taking any chances.

As she lay in bed that night, she considered the options that might lead her to more information on her family. She could go to Clarabelle's house again and try to reconnect with her ghost. But the last time she'd talked about the past, her questions and comments had upset Clarabelle. She had no desire to do that again unless she was going to tell her she'd be purchasing the house with all the new money coming her way.

Or, Hazel could take a chance and ask the town librarian Timothy Franklin if she could view the special collection of historical books and see if she could glean any information there. She'd hesitated to do that in the past because she didn't want to draw any extra attention to herself and her interest in the ancient witches, so maybe she should wait a little longer.

Perhaps her best option might be to visit with her friend Cora who she'd recently discovered was also a witch. Cora seemed to hold information close to her chest, but the past events at Redemption Pond might be something she'd be willing to discuss. If nothing else, maybe she could help her find the pond because Hazel had been unable to locate the darned place with her phone's navigation.

Perhaps her connection to Earth, might encourage nature to fill her in on some details and let her know which direction to look for more.

CHAPTER THREE

The next morning, the lottery people had yet to knock on Hazel's door. She snorted as she dressed for the day. She supposed she would have needed to purchase a lottery ticket for money to find her that way. As much as she wanted to rake in millions, she had her doubts about that spell.

Still, she remained on alert as she walked toward Cora's Café, waiting for opportunity to pop up and make her rich. Hazel and her new bestie had decided they would walk together three mornings a week after the café's breakfast crowd had dissipated and Hazel's assistant had shown up to cover the teashop.

Walking seemed to be Hazel's best solution to being able to eat all of Cora's cherry macaroons that she wanted. Since Cora was the one to make the delicious little temptations that Hazel couldn't resist, it seemed fair that Cora should support her new exercise routine.

As Hazel approached the café, she found Belinda, Cora's server with the over-inflated self-image standing outside the door with her boyfriend. Belinda flicked her long, dark hair over her shoulder and then pointed a sharp finger at Charlie Rossler who towered over her by a good five inches. From the look on her boyfriend's face, he was none too happy.

Hazel drew closer, not wanting to intrude, but unable to keep from wondering what they argued about. Neither of them looked at her as she approached the door to Cora's. Belinda held a stony expression, but her demeanor was nothing compared to Charlie's red-faced and tight expression.

He clenched his fists. "What do you think Glenys will have to say about this? You know she'll be pissed."

Belinda exhaled, smiled, and placed her hand against his chest. "Look, Charlie. I know this isn't what you want, but it is what it is. Our love affair was incredible, and I'll never forget you, but sadly, the flame has died. You need to accept that it's over."

Hazel widened her eyes and focused on the door handle as she reached for it. She'd run smack into the middle of a difficult and uncomfortable breakup scene. One she wanted no part of.

She pulled open the door and hurried inside.

The cozy diner with gleaming golden oak floors and walnut tables was a calm contrast to the scene outside. Cora waved from the back counter. The ambiance in Cora's space always greeted Hazel with a warm welcome. No wonder the café owner had no trouble keeping her tables full.

Sweet Mr. Virgil Fletcher's eyes lit up as Hazel neared his table. "Morning, Miss Hazel."

Hazel paused next to him, trying to avoid focusing on his toothless grin. The elderly man refused to wear his teeth, but from the looks of his nearly empty plate, he seemed to do fine without them. "Good morning, Mr. Fletcher. Looks like you're enjoying your breakfast."

He nodded in satisfaction. "Miss Cora makes the best food in town. That's why I come here every day."

Indeed, he did. "Where's your grandson?" The thirty-something man lived with his grandpa, and everyone in town called Quentin a saint. Hazel was glad the elderly man had someone to take care of him.

Mr. Fletcher shook his head in a dismissive way. "He's got other things to do this morning besides bothering with me. He's always working on them crazy computing things he's got. But he's a good boy."

Hazel chuckled at his reference to Quentin's job as a computer programmer. The older man suffered from a bit of dementia, but not enough that he couldn't fully enjoy his life. In fact, things rarely bothered him, so he was probably happier than most. And he was lucky that Quentin could work from home and be around to care for him if he needed it.

"Yes, Quentin is a good man." She glanced toward Cora who motioned her over. "I need to be on my way now. Cora's waiting for me, but you have yourself a good morning, okay?"

He gave her a fierce salute, and she wondered if he'd served in the military during his younger days. "Will do, ma'am."

She left him with a smile and headed to the back counter. "Ready to go?"

Cora beamed. "Just about. I'm waiting for Belinda to come back from her break."

Hazel slid onto the brown leather seat of one of the shiny silver stools along the counter and waited. A few people wanting an early lunch sat in booths and at tables, but for the most part, the place was empty.

Hazel pushed her unruly auburn curls away from her face. "She's just outside the front door. With Charlie. Arguing."

Cora drew her brows together in a worried look. "Again? That's the third time this week."

Hazel rolled her eyes. "Sounds like there's trouble in paradise. I'd like to feel sorry for her, but from my perspective, she seems to bring most of her trouble on herself." Especially with her condescending looks and quite-often snippy attitude.

Her friend gave her an understanding smile. "I know you don't like her, and I know she can be a handful, but I have to take pity and help her where I can."

"Why? I don't think she appreciates how good you are to her."

Cora shrugged. "She and I are alone in the world, discarded by our families for our abilities and beliefs." She stopped, wide-eyed, and pressed her lips together.

Hazel's jaw dropped in surprise. "You mean, she's a *wi...*" She quickly cut off what she was about to utter.

Cora blanched. "Please don't say anything to anyone. I shouldn't have let that slip."

Hazel shook her head several times. "Of course. I won't breathe a word."

Her friend still seemed concerned. "I guess it came out because I trust you so much."

Hazel tried an earnest expression. "Really. I promise. I know how important this is, and I won't say anything."

Cora relaxed a little. "You have to understand, Hazel. She has no one to help her or teach her. You've had your mother and your aunts to guide you and support you your whole life." Moisture glistened in Cora's eyes, and she quickly blinked it away.

Hazel sensed Cora's ability to whisk away her emotions, and figured it was a skill she'd had to teach herself to keep her feelings hidden so that she could stay strong. She wanted to reach out and hug her friend, but she'd found that many times people were turned off or offended by her ability to see through their thin veneers so she refrained. "Yes, the Blessed Mother did grant me a wonderful childhood."

Still, just because Cora and Belinda had shared a similar upbringing didn't mean Cora should be loyal to Belinda regardless of her behavior. But, she wouldn't argue that with her friend for now.

The door to the café swung open, and Belinda stormed in. She might have looked cool and composed outside, but whatever Charlie had said to her in the meantime had changed Belinda's whole demeanor. Cora's server walked past them without acknowledgment and pushed through the swinging door into the kitchen.

Hazel met Cora's gaze with a questioning one of her own.

Once again, Cora tried to give her a reassuring smile, even though Hazel sensed the uncertainty churning beneath. "Give me a minute to grab a jacket, and we can be on our way."

Hazel was sure Cora was going to do more than get her jacket as she headed into the kitchen, but she supposed it was kind of Cora to care about the girl.

A few minutes later, Cora returned, her expression neutral. "She's coming out, and we can go."

Together she and Hazel headed toward the door. Cora reached forward to push it open, but her hand never touched the metal bar as someone pulled it from the other side. The grandson of the toothless Mr. Fletcher, all six-foot-four-inches of Quentin Fletcher, filled the door.

He stopped seconds before barreling into them. His thinning dark hair looked as though he had run his hands through it one too many times, and the dark circles under his eyes gave him an unhealthy look. "Where is she?"

Cora blinked, looking surprised. "Where is who?"

Anger and anxiety rolled off him in waves, and Hazel put her hand on Cora's elbow as though to warn her that he was in a dangerous mood.

Quentin narrowed his eyes in anger. "That witch, Belinda." He glanced over their heads, searching the café.

Hazel cringed at his flagrant use of the word.

Cora shook her head in admonishment. "Now, Quentin, you know we can't toss those accusations out so lightly. I don't know what Belinda has done to make you so angry, but I'm sure if you calm down, we can discuss it with her and figure things out."

"I appreciate what you're trying to do Cora, but that witch has gone too far this time." He jerked his chin up in recognition and shoved past them. Hazel turned in time to see Belinda notice Quentin marching directly for her, and she widened her eyes into ovals.

She froze for a moment, but as he neared, she swiveled toward the door that led into the kitchen. Quentin grabbed her arm and jerked her back before she could disappear inside.

Quentin's anger boiled like a screaming teakettle. "Don't you run from me, you deceitful little witch."

Hazel and Cora rushed forward, reaching them just as Belinda jerked her arm free from his grasp. "Don't touch me again, or you'll regret it."

Quentin pointed a condemning finger at Belinda. "You've stolen money from my grandpa for the last time."

Cora inhaled in surprise. "What's this, Quentin? You think Belinda has stolen money?"

Belinda shook her head vehemently. "That's a big, fat lie."

"It's not a lie," Quentin yelled.

He filled his lungs. "Yesterday, I discovered that my grandpa has withdrawn fifty dollars almost every day this week. When I questioned him this morning, he didn't remember visiting the bank, but he said something about helping out a pretty little filly."

Belinda took a step back. "That doesn't mean it's me."

"He couldn't remember Belinda's name, but he gave me a description," Quentin said, ignoring her comment. "It took me a while to figure out who he was talking about, but when I checked again with the bank, they'd said that he had been dropping in first thing in the morning. He always has breakfast at Cora's, so I put two and two together."

He pointed a condemning finger at Belinda. *"It's you."*

Belinda dropped her jaw in disgusted surprise, but Hazel sensed a touch of deception there as well. "I didn't steal anything from him."

"Belinda?" Cora eyed her employee with concern. "Did you take money from Mr. Fletcher?"

Belinda looked as though she'd been caught in a liar's trap. "I didn't ask him for money, and I didn't steal anything from him. Yes, he's left me some nice tips, but I didn't ask him to, and that's his prerogative."

Cora closed her eyes for several long moments as though she was digesting this information and deciding what to do. "Belinda, you know Mr. Fletcher struggles with his ability to see rationalization."

Belinda shook her head. "Actually, I have no idea what he struggles with. That's not my concern. If Quentin doesn't trust his grandpa with his own money, then maybe he shouldn't let him wander the town unattended."

Hazel and everyone else in the room knew Belinda lied about Mr. Fletcher's mental capacity. For several years now, he had declined, and the town all watched out for him. Except, Belinda, it seemed.

Cora shook her head in disappointment, and then she faced Quentin. "I'm very sorry that someone in my employ took advantage of your grandfather while he was here. I can promise you that will never happen again."

Quentin glared at Belinda. "What about the money that she's already taken? I want it back."

Cora lifted a sharp brow and focused on Belinda, her expectations clear.

Belinda twisted her features into an angry frown. "You can't prove that he gave me every drop of money he took out of the bank.

And what he did give me was a gesture of his appreciation for me taking care of him, like you never do."

His anger leaned toward an explosion. "I take care of him every day."

"If you're taking such great care of him, then how come he can go to the bank and withdraw however much money he wants, and then wander around town until he finds his way to Cora's? Huh? When he's in here, I make him laugh and smile, and talk to him like he says you never do. If you are caring for him like you should, he wouldn't have had that opportunity."

Quentin stiffened. "I want that money back."

Belinda placed her hand on her hip and jutted it out. "Well, I don't have it. I used it for rent and groceries." She gave him a flippant smile and then turned her back and walked into the kitchen.

He shifted his anger to Cora "She's a liar," he growled. "If you're not going to do something about her, I will."

Cora placed a calming hand on his arm. "Now, Quentin, don't be acting all crazy. Give me some time, and I'll do what I can to sort this out and get Virgil's money back. Maybe Belinda can work some extra shifts, and I will put that money toward it."

Quentin seemed only slightly appeased. "You'd better."

With that, he turned and strode toward his grandpa's table. "Get up. We're going home."

Mr. Fletcher glanced about the room, looking confused. "Okay." He slowly got to his feet. When he was ready, Quentin marched from the café, leaving his grandpa to shuffle after him.

Hazel turned her gaze to Cora. "Oh, wow. That was...unexpected."

"Yeah." Cora released a long sigh.

"Perhaps we should cancel this morning's walk?" Though Hazel had really been looking forward to it.

"Maybe. Let me check on Belinda."

Cora was gone for all of five minutes. When she returned, she glanced at the clock hanging over the door. "Belinda says she'll be fine, though I can tell she's upset. Whether it's from what happened with Charlie or Quentin, I have no clue, but she's insisting that we go. Julie will be here in forty-five minutes, and I doubt Quentin will be back. I guess we should go as planned."

"If you're sure?"

Cora gave her an exasperated look. "I'm sure that I need to get out in the fresh air before I lose my mind, too. Then I can deal with the situation later. Belinda doesn't want to talk about it, but she's going to have to."

Hazel shrugged and led the way outside.

CHAPTER FOUR

Hazel and Cora left the café and walked several minutes in silence with warm April sunshine raining down on them. By degrees, Hazel sensed Cora's anxiety level falling, and she was relieved. Stress was never a good thing.

In Hazel's opinion, Belinda was a huge source of it. "I hate to say it, but maybe you should fire her. You know it's only a matter of time before everyone in town hears about what happened. You don't want your business to suffer because of her."

Cora cast a frustrated glance at her. "I can't do that, Hazel. Besides, if I fire her, you know Belinda will never repay him. If she stays working for me, then I think I can convince her to do the right thing."

If the darkness in Belinda's aura was any kind of clue, she doubted that would happen. "If you say so."

Cora sighed. "Let's not talk about her right now. I want to enjoy the morning."

Hazel did as well.

They followed their regular path down the cobblestone sidewalk and turned before they reached the police station. Hazel wasn't sure if Cora knew she'd chosen a route that wouldn't pass by Peter's place of work on purpose, but that couldn't be helped.

Hazel had found herself growing more drawn to the attractive police chief with all those amazing muscles, his dark hair and mesmerizing green eyes. But seeing him sent her pulse racing and jumbled her thoughts, and she didn't want that to interrupt the peacefulness of their morning walks.

This was her time to focus on herself and reconnect with nature.

They walked until they reached the glorious red-brick church that had sat on the corner of Camden and Oakwood for the past two hundred years. The pitched black roof and accompanying spire rose high into the sky, and she adored its arched decorative designs and windows. It seemed everything built during current times lacked the character of these old buildings, and she found that sad.

Through her research, she'd discovered the structure had been built on the same spot as the original Stonebridge church that had been in existence during her grandmother's time. That old wooden church, the place where the pious people had once condemned Clarabelle, had burned to the ground two years to the day after they'd drowned her grandmother and her friends in Redemption Pond.

She couldn't help but wonder if there was a correlation.

Cora filled her lungs with fresh air and expelled it as though cleansing the taste of their uncomfortable conversation from her mouth. "You'd be surprised how many people request your tea, Hazel. Happy Day is now almost as popular as Majestic Mint."

Pleasure wrapped around her heart. "Happy Day has become my new favorite, too. When I first thought about combining oranges, hibiscus and lemongrass, I knew it would taste good, but I'm surprised how much I like it."

"You're a master of your trade."

A modest laugh escaped Hazel. "I don't know if I would go that far." But she had learned a lot from her mother and her aunts about brews and potions, and tea had become her passion.

"Don't try to argue that with me and the community. We all love what you do."

Hazel nodded in satisfaction. As much as the anti-witch town should dislike her, she'd begun to feel like she belonged to the community. As long as she kept her heritage a secret. "That makes me really happy."

Cora pumped her elbows for a greater workout. "You give the customers what they want. Makes us all happy."

Hazel had tried to focus on the beautiful day and all that the Blessed Mother offered them, but she couldn't escape the annoying reminder of her evening before and the spells she'd read. Cora believed Hazel came from a long line of good witches, and Hazel didn't want to tell her otherwise.

At least not yet. Their friendship had deepened over the past several weeks, and Hazel was grateful that she had a confidante in town, but she wasn't sure she wanted to share her family's sordid past and chance Cora thinking less of her.

Still, she yearned to know more about her grandmother and the things that had taken place all those years ago. She battled between speaking what was on her mind or keeping it to herself. In the end, her heart won, like it usually did, but maybe shouldn't have. "Can I pick your brain?"

Cora graced her with a friendly smile "Sure."

"How much do you know about what happened to the witches at Redemption Pond?"

Cora widened her eyes. "Oh. That."

She'd opened the can of worms now, so she might as well push forward. "I've been researching, reading what I can find in books, but everything I've found has been biased toward the townsfolk."

"Books from the library?" Cora asked cautiously.

Hazel nodded, understanding the warning in her voice. It hadn't taken Hazel long to realize the town's librarian held a special hatred toward witches. "I've been careful not to seem too eager in front of Timothy. He mentioned the special books that I can only review in his presence, and I've been holding back asking to see them."

"Smart thinking. Wait a while first. I've heard there's a diary of one of the witches who was sentenced to die that day."

Something in her voice caught Hazel's attention. "Sentenced to die? You make it sound like they didn't actually go through with it."

The smile wrinkles in her cheeks deepened. "Oh. Of course. You wouldn't know."

Hazel drew her brows together in confusion. "I wouldn't know what?"

Cora pulled her to a stop and met her gaze. "Those witches didn't die that day."

Her words sent Hazel's thoughts into a chaotic frenzy. "What do you mean they didn't die?" Her grandmother had lived? "I thought the townsfolk sentenced them to death, rowed them out into the middle of Redemption Pond, and cast them overboard with their hands tied behind their backs and stones in their pockets."

A gentle breeze tugged a strand of hair across Cora's face, and she pushed it out of the way. "That's all very true. Once the witches were all in the water, the fine citizens of Stonebridge returned to their homes. The next day though, the witches and all the water in Redemption Pond were gone. Vanished. Evaporated. A mystery they couldn't explain."

Her stomach twisted into an anxious knot. *Clarabelle's spell had worked?* "That's incredible." And a little frightening. She'd known her ancestor had been powerful, but...

She tried to imagine the amount of energy a feat like that would take. Unfathomable. Hazel couldn't even manage a simple glamour or money spell.

"The righteous folks told themselves the devil had come to claim them, and all the water evaporated because of the fires of hell." She snorted.

"If they didn't die, what happened to them?"

Cora shrugged. "There are many guesses, but no one knows for sure. Some think they escaped and went in search of their families who'd fled. Others said they lived in the woods next to Clarabelle's house for a time, planning their revenge before they disappeared."

"Hence, the yearly Witch's Wrath storm we endured not long ago?"

"Could be. Most witches today don't believe anyone could create a spell that powerful. But none of us really know."

Except Hazel did. She'd read the powerful spell that had created the mother of all storms, and she yearned to know more. "I'd really like to see Redemption Pond. How far is it?"

"It's about a mile off the main road as you head out of town from the north. It's not a huge body of water, but still decent-sized. The non-superstitious folks like to paddle around it in canoes and rowboats. It's a gorgeous place. Hard to believe something so tragic happened there."

Hazel chuckled. Stonebridge was truly a conundrum. "Is there anywhere in town that's not gorgeous?"

"True." Cora nodded her head in agreement. "It makes me laugh to know some in town still refuse to go anywhere near it because they think the devil might get them, too. Others say it's haunted with the witches' spirits."

Her pulse increased. "Is it?"

"Not that I've ever seen, but I try to avoid places that have anything to do with the witches from the past. I don't want to draw unnecessary attention."

"That's always a worry for me, too." She sighed as she searched for a way to make a visit to the pond work.

A slow grin spread across Cora's face and made her nervous. "I have an idea that would keep you safe."

Hazel knew exactly what she'd say. "Peter."

"Yes. What better cover than that broad-shouldered, handsome police chief you've been seeing? You wouldn't be the first couple to sneak out to Redemption Pond for a lover's tryst."

Heat crept into Hazel's cheeks. "We're not lovers." Hazel would never be able to let things progress that far.

"Yet," Cora returned.

In a perfect world where people didn't carry prejudices, she dreamed of falling in love with Peter. But that wasn't her world, and he could never truly love someone like her. "We've been on three dates, and those weren't exactly official," Hazel countered.

Cora arched an intrigued brow. "Some people do it on the first date."

Hazel snorted and shook her head. "We are not having this conversation."

She chuckled. "Okay, we'll save it for another day. But, I'm still going to push for a date at the pond with your handsome man. I'll even pack the picnic. I happen to know Chief Parrish loves my roast beef sandwiches."

It did sound like fun and would give her the perfect excuse for being there.

"I'll pack extra pickles for you," Cora teased.

The temptation of Cora's homemade dill pickles decided it for her. "Deal. I'll call him when I'm back at my shop."

The moment she spoke her agreement, her stomach dropped. Even though she and Peter had been on several dates, and she'd been around him plenty during his investigations, the thought of asking him out terrified her.

Still if she wanted to learn more, she would have to be braver.

She'd dared to move to a town that hated her kind. She could certainly ask a man to join her for lunch.

CHAPTER FIVE

Hazel paced her living room, her nerves a bunch of tangled vines. She'd been ready for her picnic date with Peter an hour ago, and now had nothing to do except try to plan a day she couldn't control and then worry.

Mr. Kitty released a loud sigh from where he was perched on the back of the couch. She shot him an irritated look. "If you were the one about to go on a date with someone who despised the magic in your blood, you'd be nervous, too."

Her cat only stared, leaving her to feel like she needed to defend her choices

"Yes, I should probably stop seeing Peter, but Clarabelle didn't seem to have a problem with him." Or at least that was the impression she'd gotten from her grandmother's ghost.

Mr. Kitty stood and stretched before he jumped off the couch and left the room. She had the distinct impression that he wasn't the type of feline who would stick around while she crashed and burned. Cora had said he might help her and protect her, but she had to wonder. As far as she could tell, he barely tolerated her. She'd been lucky he hadn't outed her to Peter that day at Clarabelle's house.

Maybe, if she studied the spell book more, that would appease the darned cat. But the idea that her grandmother's evaporation spell had worked made her more nervous than before.

The knock on her front door startled her, drawing her from her worried thoughts. *Peter.* Just his name rolling through her mind sent her heart racing faster.

At the door, she paused to draw in a deep, calming breath and released it before she turned the knob.

For all the good it did her.

If she'd thought the town's police chief looked incredibly attractive in his uniform, the sight of him in a light gray Henley, faded jeans, and hiking boots left her head spinning. They'd been out together before for things like root beer floats or an impromptu meeting at the sacred Grove next to Clarabelle's house, but this was their very first official date.

The smile that crossed Peter's lips devastated her. "Hey," he said.

A burst of warm happiness blossomed on her lips, and she stepped back to let him enter. "Hey," she said in return. "This might be the first time I've seen you out of uniform."

He drew his brows together in thought. "Really?"

She nodded. "Mmm-hmm."

"And?" he prompted.

"And...you look nice." Better than nice, but she couldn't tell him that.

He grinned. "Well, you look perfect."

She wasn't sure anyone had ever used the word "perfect" when describing her, and his compliment tugged hard on her heartstrings. "Stop, or you'll make me blush."

"That's the idea."

Not knowing how to respond, she smiled and shook her head. "Let me grab our lunch from the fridge, and I'll be ready."

Though she hadn't invited him to, he followed her into the kitchen. "I like what you've done with the place. It's definitely you."

She pulled the boxed lunches from the fridge, slid them into her backpack and then turned toward him. "How do you mean?"

He shrugged. "I don't know." He glanced about the room. "It's fresh and charming with a hint of mystery."

She chuckled. "Mystery? You think I'm mysterious?"

"In a good way." He took the backpack from her hands and then held out his elbow for her.

She slipped her fingers around his arm, absorbing his electrifying touch. Physically and emotionally, she sensed his strength, and she liked it. That right there could lead her down a long road of trouble. She would need to be careful.

Together, they walked to her front door. She spotted Mr. Kitty in his favorite spot beneath the couch, and quickly closed the door behind them. He had a creepy way of stalking her, and she mentally challenged him to keep up with her this time. It was one thing for him to follow her on her bicycle to Clarabelle's house which really wasn't that far away. But Redemption Pond was much farther than that, and she and Peter would be going by—

"Is that your truck?"

A shiny black Dodge was parked along the curb outside her house. If trucks could be sexy then this one would be the sexiest.

Peter chuckled. "What? Did you think I only drove the police cruiser? I do have a life outside of my job."

Her cheeks heated in embarrassment. "Of course, you do." Seeing him as a police chief made it easy to think of him as invincible, including any damage she might do to his heart. But as a man, being with him seemed so much more...intimate.

The trip to Redemption Pond took them no more than ten minutes. The area was crowded with trees, so many maples, oaks and pines, that it made it impossible to see the pond from the road. The bright and sunny Sunday afternoon had lured a fair number of brave people to the pond, enough that the small dirt parking lot was filled with cars.

Peter parked and assisted her from his truck, once again tossing her backpack filled with their lunch and a soft blanket over his shoulder.

As they began walking, he took her hand without asking. She smiled at the gesture and appreciated that they had grown more comfortable with each other.

The quote from her grandmother's book of spells popped into her mind. *Better to follow your heart, or you're already dead.*

Once again, she pondered her grandmother's thoughts behind those words. Had that been an encouragement for her grandmother to be bold, to not be afraid to use dark magic? Even though Clarabelle had used spells Hazel would never touch, she'd decided to believe it wasn't out of malice, but for her protection instead.

Better to follow your heart. Hmm...

Was that what she was doing here with Peter? Following her heart? Would dating him lead her down a similar dangerous path toward a bad ending?

She found it hard to believe such a thing while walking on a peaceful dirt trail that disappeared into a cluster of elegant trees and while holding the warm, strong hand of a man she liked. She remembered the promise she'd made before she'd come to Stonebridge to not allow her fears or her mother's fears to stop her from living.

If she did, she might as well be dead, too.

Maybe that's what Clarabelle had meant.

Peter squeezed her hand, drawing her thoughts to him. "Thanks for the invite today. I don't know if Bartles likes working the Sunday shift, but he's the one always telling me I need to relax more and enjoy life. So, here I am."

She smiled up at him, enjoying the sparks of electrified attraction coursing between their clasped hands. "Well, either way he's right. Everyone needs to take time away from work and the hassles of life. Otherwise, we become unbalanced and no longer happy."

He exhaled and gave a thoughtful nod. "Yeah, you're right. That's something I'm definitely guilty of since my wife died."

She wanted to say murdered, because his wife had died by nefarious means, a hit-and-run accident where the culprit was never found, but she couldn't. Did losing someone that way make grieving impossible to complete?

She wanted to know so much about him, but it was hard to ask a man about his past life when it involved tragedy. Still, if they were to become good friends, then they would have to learn to be open with each other.

She hoped her question wouldn't ruin their beautiful day, but he had been the one to bring her up, so maybe it was okay. "Can I ask about her? Your wife?"

The air between them tightened, and he gripped her hand tighter in response. His pain was present, but she didn't feel it was unbearably so. More like a heaviness, without being too burdensome. He'd obviously experienced a fair amount of healing in the time since his wife had been stolen from him.

"What do you want to know?"

She hesitated not sure what she wanted to ask about this woman Peter had loved so deeply. "I don't know. Maybe what was her name? What did she look like? What made you fall in love with her, if that's not too hard to answer."

The tension between them eased slightly, and she was grateful. "Her name was Sarah. She had long auburn hair like yours, though hers was straight. In some ways, you remind me a lot of her."

"Is that why you always flirt with me?"

He turned his gaze toward her, his beautiful green eyes piercing deep into her soul. "No, I don't think so. You have some similarities, but you are two separate, distinct people in my mind."

Hazel's heart lightened. She had needed to know that he was interested in her for herself and that she wasn't a ghost of his previous life. "What do you find similar about us?"

He smiled then, and the gesture was like a burst of sunshine through the dappled shade from the overhead trees. "You both love the outdoors, and you're quick to smile. And you both care about others."

She nodded. She supposed that did sound like her. "She seems like she was a great lady."

He nodded thoughtfully. "She was."

They emerged from the trees onto a peaceful meadow. A soft breeze blew over the grass, causing a wave of greens and yellows. The area didn't hold the same magical quality as Clarabelle's sacred grove, but it was beyond beautiful all the same. "This is breathtaking."

It was hard to imagine the travesty that had taken place there over three hundred years ago. But she supposed time really did heal all things. Those who'd let their fears keep them from coming to such a lovely place were really missing out.

"It is a beautiful spot," he said. "I tried to leave Stonebridge behind when I was younger, but I've never found any place that compares. I haven't been out here in a while other than patrols around the outer perimeter. I forget how amazing it is."

"Cora said a lot people don't want to come out here because of past tragedies."

He caught her gaze and held. "Past tragedies? I guess you could call them that."

An unwelcome reminder of their differences pinched her. She ignored the sting in her heart. "I find it hard to believe people today still cling to those superstitions."

He shrugged. "Some people can be crazy in their thinking."

He slowed, stopped, and turned around. "Will you look at that?" He pointed off to the side of her.

She followed his gaze. A five-dollar bill fluttered beneath a rock several steps away, and her jaw dropped in surprise.

Peter released her hand long enough to retrieve it, and he handed it to her. "A memento of our first date."

"Oh, thanks." A small thrill skittered through her. Then, as she pondered her ability to draw money to her, she realized the joke was on her. A drop of blood on a penny generated five dollars. If she wanted millions, she'd be looking at a bank robbery and a massacre.

As they neared the pond, which seemed big enough to be called a lake in her estimation, they crossed a trail of dirt tire tracks. "I thought cars couldn't get back here."

He chuckled. "There's a private access road the town put in a few years ago, but they keep it closed to the public to maintain the serenity of the area. Motorized vehicles of any kind are prohibited unless authorized."

She grinned. "You sound so official. Is that coming from the police chief or my date?"

He smiled but didn't reply and slipped the backpack from his shoulder. He gestured toward the grassy spot before them that offered a beautiful view of the pond. "How about here?"

"Looks perfect to me."

A sparkle twinkled in his eyes. "Me, too." But he wasn't looking at the pond, and her heart did a little flip in response. She should have known she couldn't have resisted such a man. She needed to face the fact that she was in deep enough she couldn't leave him without incurring a great deal of heartbreak.

CHAPTER SIX

Peter handed the backpack to Hazel and spread the turquoise and green quilt her grandmother had handstitched for her on the fresh grass. Together, they sat, both facing the pond. A delicious hum coursed through her veins, and she appreciated her happiness despite their unknown future.

He inhaled deeply. "Dang if it's not as beautiful as a fresh peach pie today."

Peach pie? She held back a snicker. She supposed pies could be beautiful, but she'd never heard anyone compare them to beautiful scenery before.

He dragged the backpack toward him and unzipped it. "Let's see what you brought us. I've been wondering ever since you pulled it out of the fridge."

His excitement was infectious. "I'm not sure, either. Cora wanted to surprise us. Though I think you will like her choice of sandwiches."

He widened his eyes, pleased. "That can only mean roast beef." He pulled out a closed white box and handed it to her before he removed a second one. He proceeded to open his, inspecting the offerings one by one.

Hazel opened hers, too, but watched what he laid in front of him.

He opened the sandwich wrapper. "Just as I suspected. Roast beef, my favorite." He lifted plastic lids from two short Styrofoam cups. "Grapes, and heaven help me, Cora's potato salad."

He opened a small brown sack and peeked inside. "Cherry macaroons for dessert."

She groaned in delight. "Oh, yum. Now, those are my favorite."

He pulled half of his sandwich from its wrapper. "It looks like she packed us a heck of a lunch. I say we dig in."

She had absolutely no problem with that.

They ate their food in companionable peace, and she gave him a brief recounting of the incidents with Belinda at Cora's diner, including what happened with Charlie and Quentin.

Peter stuck his fork into the potato salad. "Cora should just fire her."

"That's what I said, but she doesn't want to. She feels sorry for Belinda and seems protective. Cora thinks if she stays in her life, she can have a greater influence over her and maybe help her."

Peter shrugged but seemed dubious. "I guess it doesn't hurt to try, but I've seen people who sacrificed their happiness repeatedly to help those who don't want help and who refuse to change."

She pondered his words for a moment. "Sounds like you think people can't change their thoughts or actions."

He gave her a doubtful look. "Some can, if they really want to. But most people either don't want to or aren't willing to give it the effort."

She paused and uncertainty rolled through her. "What about you?" she asked as innocently as she could. "Are you the kind of guy who's open to listening to other points of view? Or are you pretty certain about your view of the world?"

He trapped her gaze as he swallowed and then took a drink of his bottled ice tea. "I like to think I have an open mind." He watched her with interested eyes for another few seconds. "Are you referring to anything in particular?"

She widened her eyes into innocent ovals and shook her head. "No. Just curious."

He tilted his head. "What about you?"

She had no problem answering that. "I'm accepting of anyone and anything as long as others aren't harmed."

"Hmm..." He nodded with what seemed like approval. "It's good to have an open mind, I guess."

She lifted a cherry macaroon. "I like to think so." Then she sank her teeth into its deliciousness. "Oh, my goodness. These are heaven."

He chuckled. "You like them that much?"

She nodded as she stuffed the other half into her mouth. "I would kill for these."

He lifted a sexy brow. "Don't do that, or I'll have to arrest you."

She laughed. "It would be worth it."

He glanced at his bag of cookies and then the other half of her uneaten sandwich. "I'll trade you my cookies for the rest of your sandwich."

She didn't hesitate for a second. "Deal."

They chatted and flirted as they finished their meal. When they'd piled the remains of the lunch into the backpack, he stretched out on his back, glancing up toward the birds squawking overhead. "We need to do this more often."

Her heart squeezed in agreement and shut down the voice that said it might not be a good idea. "We should."

He shifted his gaze to her but only smiled. And dang if it wasn't a smile that melted her ever-loving heart. Blessed Mother help her.

"That cloud looks like an elephant, don't you think?" he asked.

Not yet comfortable lying right beside him, she rested on one elbow and turned her gaze upward. "Where?"

He snorted. "You can't really watch the clouds from that position." He patted his stomach. "Lay down and put your head here. I promise I won't bite."

She acted like what he'd asked didn't make her pulse race, and she laid perpendicular to him, resting her head on his rock-solid abs.

His fingers grazed her cheek, trailing toward her chin, sending shivers racing through her. With a gentle touch, he turned her head to the right. "Straight up there. Four thick legs, and you can see his trunk."

White, fluffy clouds danced across the brilliant blue sky, and she searched them for what he described. "I can't...wait, I see it."

"Good." He chuckled, the act causing her head to bounce with him. "See anything else?"

She flicked her gaze from one puff of white to another, looking for familiar shapes as his chest expanded and contracted with each breath. The feel of his fingers brushing her hair distracted her, and when he tugged on several strands, she could no longer focus on the sky. Only the sensation of his soft touch.

She couldn't be sure, but she imagined he twined one of her curls around and around his finger. The act was tender and endearing, and by slow degrees, she relaxed against him. This man who didn't approve of witches made her feel the safest she ever had.

By now, Victor, would have ignored the clouds and her desires, and gone straight for what made him feel good. Funny how she'd thought she'd loved him so much. She couldn't deny their energy had been potent. But where Victor had been a white-hot flash in the pan, what she experienced with Peter was more a delicious sensation that she knew could deepen into something strong, sexy and wonderful if she could allow it.

Which she couldn't, but it was nice to think about.

And no one said she couldn't enjoy this time with him right now.

"Your hair is really soft." His voice sounded distant, almost sleepy. She wanted to turn to check his expression, but her highly-sensitized emotions kept her from looking.

So, she remained quiet, allowing his steady breaths to lull her into a relaxed state. She closed her eyes for a moment, reveling in the feel of his fingers in her hair.

The sound of a bird squawking woke her with a start. She opened her eyes and cast a glance toward the pond. A duck lifted from the water and flapped higher into the air, heading for grass on the opposite side of the pond from where she and Peter lay.

His breaths remained steady and deep, and she was sure he'd fallen asleep, too. She carefully sat up and turned to face him. His features were relaxed, and the hand that had played with her hair now rested against his chest.

She found it impossible to not visually trace the curve of his pecs beneath his light gray cotton Henley. Even in sleep, he was imposing. And irresistible.

She sat for a few moments watching him, studying the dark fan of eyelashes resting near his cheekbones. She drew an imaginary finger over the curve of his lips and shivered when she remembered how she'd felt the last time he'd kissed her.

This thing between them was strong. Strong enough it should scare her. And, well, it did. But not enough to make her run the other direction. Part of her believed she could handle things and maintain her secrets. Another part desperately wanted to trust Clarabelle's approval of him. She didn't want to consider any negative thoughts she harbored.

She wasn't sure if that made her smart...or stupid.

After staring long enough to make her feel like a creeper, she opted for a walk along the edge of the pond. She'd come to this place to learn more or at least see if she could sense any residual energy from the past. She knew she would have had a harder time if Peter was awake, but his restful slumber provided her the perfect opportunity.

She carefully stood and inched her way from him, opting for soft footsteps until she was sure she wouldn't wake him. She wouldn't go far. He'd be able to see her if he woke. But for now, she'd allow him the rest he obviously needed. The man worked too hard.

Not far from where she approached the edge of the water was a short wooden dock. She couldn't imagine what it might be used for, other than maybe fishing.

She tested the strength of the weathered wood before she put her full weight on it and walked forward. The last thing she wanted was a dip in the green-tinted water fully dressed.

At the end of the dock, she stopped and allowed her senses to drink in the beauty of life displayed before her. Dragonflies swooped and dipped above the smooth surface of the water, while beneath, quick flashes of small fish darted by. She imagined some of the less fortunate dragonflies would become lunch for the fish. Such was the circle of life.

Hazel smiled, silently thanking the Blessed Mother for the beauty she'd created. She opened her hands outward as far as she could without seeming awkward or suspicious. Inhaling a cleansing breath, she closed her eyes and tipped her face toward the sun. Warmth caressed her skin, and she opened her senses.

Calm serenity greeted her with a loving embrace. The essence of life buzzed around her, and she accepted the incredible energy that cleansed her soul.

When her spirit was considerably lighter, she allowed her memories to drift to the historical accounts of what had happened so many years ago. She thought of Clarabelle and what she must have felt as villagers rowed her and her friends to the center of the lake.

Fear. Anger. Likely hatred.

She searched the atmosphere for signs of those dark, powerful emotions.

Nothing.

She remained vigilant for several more minutes, understanding that something that old might require more time and more energy.

Finally, she opened her eyes and exhaled a deep breath.

Nothing of the past remained. At least nothing she could sense, and she had powerful abilities in that area. Thankfully, there was nothing left but beauty and serenity.

Her grandmother and her friends had the capability to evaporate this amount of water. The idea of it blew her mind.

Then again, her mother had always told her dark magic should never be underestimated. Still, if she didn't have proof otherwise, she'd never believe it could happen.

Several fishermen dotted the edges of the placid pond, and she imagined this was where they chose to reconnect with spirit, even if they didn't realize it. On the far edge of the pond, two teenagers paddled across the surface, their laughs reaching out to Hazel.

Time and the Blessed Mother must have worked their magic and erased all traces of that long-ago tragedy. If only Clarabelle could do the same and find her peace.

As far as Hazel knew, she was the first of her family to return to Stonebridge. Maybe her presence and encouragement would help Clarabelle to move on to a brighter and happier place where she could return to the light and discard darkness once and for all.

She muttered a quick plea to the Blessed Mother to help her in this endeavor.

With a renewed sense of purpose burning in her heart, she turned to head back to Peter.

A wave of anguish slapped her hard, and she inhaled sharply. But this wasn't old fear. It was new, tightened, fresh and concise. With her hand over her heart, she looked back to the pond to discover the source.

The sight of an odd-shaped, large object several hundred feet out in the pond caught her attention. She squinted, her eyes fighting the glare of sunshine bouncing off the water as she tried to discern what it was.

Too big to be a fish...

Then she noticed hair fanning on the surface and gasped. Her stomach roiled as she filled her lungs, and then she screamed.

CHAPTER SEVEN

The sound of a scream pierced Peter's daydreams and brought him upright, his heart pounding. He blinked as he glanced around, trying to get his bearings.

Picnic. Hazel. Nap.

Hazel?

Panic ripped through him when he realized she was missing, and he bolted to his feet. The sight of her racing across the grass toward him should have reassured him, but the look of sheer horror on her face was a knife to his heart.

He ran toward her. When she was within reach, he caught her in his arms, halting her stride. Her breaths were short and desperate.

"Body." She breathed. "In the water." She grabbed his hand, and together, they sprinted toward the pond with Hazel leading the way.

The sound of their shoes hitting the wooden dock echoed around him. Hazel screeched to a stop and then pointed over the water. He scanned the surface, hoping she'd mistaken a shadow from the overhead clouds or debris for the body.

But, no. He spotted the object she pointed at, and dread sluiced over him like pouring rain on a cold day.

He jerked his phone from his pocket and dialed the station. Hazel watched him with eyes full of fear, and he reached for her hand to comfort her. "John. Get a unit out to Redemption Pond now. I'm out here, and we've discovered a body in the water." He hung up without waiting for a reply.

He shoved his phone into Hazel's hands and gripped the bottom of his shirt, pulling it over his head. "You should wait in my truck." He pulled off his boots, trying to remain calm despite the adrenaline flooding his veins.

She shook her head vehemently. "I want to stay. I need to know who it is."

He unbuttoned his jeans and shimmied out of them, knowing the weighted fabric would slow him down once he hit the water. "Dead bodies aren't pleasant to look at, Hazel. The sight can stay with you forever."

"I watched Mr. Winthrop die."

"That's different than a bloated body that's been in the water a while." Without waiting for her reply, he dove in, hoping she'd do as he asked.

With strong, powerful strokes, he swam across the pond, trying to focus on something other than what floated ahead of him. He couldn't wait for help to arrive if there was the slightest chance the person might be alive, but from his point of view at the dock, it was unlikely.

He wished Hazel would listen to him and stay away from what would likely be a gruesome sight, but he doubted she would.

He loved that she was made of strong material. Any woman he might consider having in his life would need to be with his line of work. Sarah had always balked at hearing about some of the events he dealt with, so he'd minimized any discussions about them with her. But sometimes, the things he witnessed ate at him, and he'd wished he could have someone to help release those burdens.

Not the guys at the station. He couldn't be vulnerable with them. But sharing with someone like Hazel would be so good for him. She had a strong will, that one.

As he approached the body, he mentally curtained off his emotions as he took in details including the long, dark hair fanned on the top of the water and the curve of a trim waist that widened at the hips.

A woman.

When his hands bumped into her body, he stopped swimming and treaded water. The woman's body bobbed, and he knew right away from the color of her skin and lack of motion that she was no longer breathing.

Peter couldn't help but think about his wife's death. Sarah hadn't died in a drowning, but he knew somewhere out there was a family whose life was about to be forever changed.

He gripped the cold arm and turned her over. Belinda's once-beautiful face greeted him with lifeless eyes, and his stomach lurched. Didn't matter how many times he dealt with dead bodies, he'd never get used to it.

Wailing sirens pierced the air, and he looked toward them, grateful that his men had made good time. He only wished he'd be bringing them a live person instead.

He steeled his nerves, grasped Belinda's body under the armpit, and began the arduous process of making his way back to shore.

He made steady progress across the pond, and slowly, the shore grew nearer. When he finally reached the dock, three men and Hazel waited for him. His officers knelt, and on the count of three, they lifted and dragged the water-logged body onto the dock.

One of his men cursed.

"Belinda Atkins," Jones said softly.

Peter met his gaze and nodded. In a small town like theirs, it was hard not to become friendly with most everyone, and Peter knew the rooky Jones had had a sweet spot for Belinda. Like most of his single male employees.

She'd served Peter coffee only yesterday. In less than twenty-four hours, she'd gone from flirtatious and bubbly to...gone. She ceased to exist in their world forevermore.

He silently said a prayer for her soul.

A despondent mood settled over him like a coroner's white sheet. "Let's get her on the gurney and try to preserve what evidence might be left. Hopefully, the coroner will be able to learn something from her to tell us what happened."

The men lifted Belinda's body and carried her toward the gurney while Peter hoisted himself onto the deck, water dripping from every part of his body. Belinda had been a looker and a flirt, and even Peter had always appreciated her smile. Yeah, she'd had her share of issues, but any loss of life before a person's time was unacceptable.

"Don't look," he said in a low voice to Hazel.

She nodded as though she agreed to his request and held out a blanket one of his men must have given her, but she didn't look away until he took her hand. Nothing he could do now about what she'd seen, but once they'd loaded Belinda on the gurney, he intended to send Hazel home with one of his men whether she liked it or not. He'd use his position as chief if necessary.

CHAPTER EIGHT

Hazel watched in shock as Peter swam to shore and the other officers lifted Belinda onto the dock. Even with damp, limp hair and a bloated body, Hazel recognized her. Her heart clutched at the unexpected, horrific loss of life.

Peter climbed out of the water, but she barely noticed the lack of most of his clothes and dripping body as she handed a blanket to him. She stepped back to let the officers pass as they carried Belinda across the short dock and placed her gently on the waiting gurney. As they did, her lifeless arm flopped over the edge and dangled downward, revealing the underneath of her bicep.

A sloppy, inverted pentagram drawn with thick, black lines looked like a stark brand against her pale, wet skin. With the sounds of the officers' voices a dim buzz in her head, Hazel moved to follow them so she could inspect the graffiti, but Peter took her hand.

She swallowed in horror. Many believed an inverted pentagram was the sign of the devil, but any witch worth her cauldron knew that wasn't true. Or at least it wasn't originally true. Modern Satanists had claimed it as their own.

Regardless, Hazel was certain that pentagram hadn't been on Belinda's arm three mornings ago when she'd found her breaking up with Charlie outside of Cora's café. She feared that meant someone had marked her as a witch before he or she had killed her. Or even after she was dead.

Peter blocked her view once again, and she glanced upward to his face. Water droplets fell from his hair, and his expression was dire. Of course, it was. He'd jumped in after Belinda like the hero he was, and she realized how disturbingly difficult his job must be at times.

"Don't look, Hazel," he repeated. "They can give you nightmares."

She nodded, allowing him to turn her from the sight of the body. She could look away, but he wouldn't be able to.

He stuffed his feet back into his boots even though his socks were soggy, and then picked up his shirt and jeans. With the blanket tucked around his hips, he grasped her hand and led her to the passenger side of one of the police units. Outside the door, he paused. "I'm going to ask Sargent Gentry to take you home."

"I want to stay." It wasn't that she wanted to see Belinda again, but the thought of going home alone after this seemed unbearable. She needed to know more, needed to talk with Peter about what had happened.

Concern reflected in his eyes. "I'm going to be here awhile, documenting notes, waiting for the coroner, interviewing witnesses."

"I could help with that."

He reached up and tugged a stray strand of hair from her face. "You know I love your help, but this is an official police investigation. You can't help right now."

She knew he was right, but that didn't make her feel any better.

He opened the passenger door of the SUV, and she had no choice but to climb inside.

"I could bring back dry clothes for you."

He gently shook his head. "One of my men can. But, there is something you can do. Go to Cora's. We both know she cared about Belinda, and this will be a hard blow for her. There are enough witnesses to ignite the gossip fire before long. You'll be doing her a kindness if you break it to her in private and give her time to prepare before the onslaught of questions and comments come her way."

Hazel closed her eyes for a long moment, imagining the pain she'd find on her friend's face when she told her. "You're right. I need to be the one to break it to her."

He nodded in agreement and then patted her leg. "I'll send Gentry right over, and he can drive you."

Knowing that she had a purpose made leaving easier. "Okay. You'll call me later?"

"I'll call you when I can." With that, he shut the door and strode away.

A few moments later, the older officer with sandy-blond hair and intense blue eyes climbed into the SUV. "Cora's Café?"

"Yes, please."

Hazel and the officer both remained silent during the ride back to town. She had a million questions, but she knew he wouldn't be able to talk to her about them, and generating everyday chit-chat to fill the void just seemed wrong.

When he pulled alongside the curb in front of the café, she grabbed her backpack and quilt and opened the door. "Thanks for the ride."

"No problem, ma'am."

She heard him pull away as she reached to open the door. Instead of entering, she paused and silently asked the Blessed Mother to give her enough strength for her and her friend because she knew Cora would have none of her own.

After taking a steadying breath, she stepped inside.

Cora looked up from behind the counter, a smile blossoming on her face when her gaze connected with Hazel. "Hey, lady," she called and motioned her over. "How about some ice cream, and you can tell me all about your hot date?"

Hazel swallowed and moved forward, circling behind the counter instead of sidling up to the opposite side like she usually did. Thankfully, only a few people occupied the booths, and Cora had hours before the dinner crowd arrived.

As Hazel neared, Cora's happy expression dropped to concern. "Oh, no. It didn't go well?"

Unexpected tears sprang to Hazel's eyes as she tried to form the appropriate words to say. She came up empty.

"Cora..." She took her hand and tugged her into the kitchen. Bernard shifted his gaze from the grill he scraped to them. Heavy-set and in his fifties, he eyed them with raised brows as though he wanted to know why they'd dared to enter his lair.

"Could we have a few minutes, Bernard?" Cora asked. She thought she was sparing Hazel from an uncomfortable moment. Little did she know...

He agreed with a dip of his head. "Sure. I need to step out back for a moment anyway."

Smoke break, Hazel thought and wiped tears from her cheeks. When the door closed behind him, Hazel took both of Cora's hands and met her gaze.

Cora must have sensed something because she started shaking her head as though she knew what was coming.

"There's been an accident." Or possibly murder, if anyone asked her. "It's Belinda."

Heartbreak exploded in Cora's eyes. "No." She gripped Hazel's hands tighter. "*No.*"

She gave her a gentle nod. "They..." Not they. "I spotted her floating in the water at Redemption Pond."

Cora shook her head rapidly and then released Hazel's hands, using the wall to steady herself instead. "That can't be right. Belinda is a good swimmer. Maybe it wasn't her."

Hazel tugged her toward a stool and forced her to sit. "It was her, Cora. I saw her. Peter did, too. He sent me to tell you before you heard it from someone else." She admired that, even in dark times, Peter thought of others.

Tears flowed unfettered now, and Cora repeatedly shook her head. "No. I can't believe it. She can't be gone."

Hazel located a box of tissues in a nearby pantry and opened it, giving Cora several. She'd likely need them and more before the day was over. "Peter doesn't have any answers yet. He was still investigating when I left, and it sounded like he'd be there a long time. But I'm sure he'll tell you what he can when he can."

"Oh, Hazel. I just can't..." Cora's voice broke on another sob, and Hazel wrapped her in a caring embrace.

"It's okay," she whispered. "Cry all you need."

"She was so young. So smart and beautiful."

"I know. I know."

Cora tilted her tear-stained face toward Hazel and sniffed. "Do you think someone found out?" she half-whispered, half-sobbed.

The image of the inverted pentagram reared in Hazel's mind, but she didn't feel she could tell Cora. At least not now. Either way, it seemed Belinda hadn't been so smart after all. "I don't know."

Cora stared, her red-rimmed eyes full of anguish, the look on her face leaving Hazel anxious. "Do you think that had something to do with her death?" Hazel asked. "Maybe one of the *others* discovered her heritage?"

"I don't know." Cora's voice hitched. "But I do know she was a darn good swimmer."

Hazel sighed and shook her head, not knowing how to process this tragedy, let alone help her friend. "I don't think you're in any shape to handle the café tonight. Is there someone I can call to cover for you?"

"Lobster Lucy." She sniffed.

Hazel still couldn't call the lovely older lady by that name, even though everyone else did.

"She ran it for a couple of days when I cut a tendon in my thumb and needed surgery," Cora continued. "Her number's in the small black book near the phone in the office."

Cora's office was really a four-by-six closet that held a small desk complete with computer, phone and a chair. There wasn't room for anything else. Hazel located Lucy's number and called her.

A few moments later, she returned to Cora to find her sobbing into her hands. Hazel grabbed more tissues and rushed forward. "I'm so sorry." She hugged her again.

"Lucy's on her way," Hazel continued. "Should be here shortly. We can walk the couple of blocks to my house, and I'll make you some wonderful tea, okay? I think you should spend the night, too. Blessed Mother knows I'm not up for being alone right now, so I'm sure you're not, either."

Cora nodded. "Thank you, Hazel. You're a good friend."

"Of course. Anything you need." Hazel might even brew Clarabelle's recipe for chamomile tea that she'd been dying to try.

CHAPTER NINE

Something soft brushed Hazel's cheek, stirring her from her sleep. She smiled at the comforting feeling and allowed drowsiness to consume her again.

More lovely caresses feathered across her face, and she struggled to discern if they were part of her dreams or came from reality. Either way, they were so nice...

Smack.

This time, the touch was not loving.

She opened her eyes abruptly and found Mr. Kitty perched atop her chest, glaring at her with impatience. She blinked a few times and then glared back. "Did you just slap me?"

He released a meow full of irritation, as though to confirm that he had indeed attacked her while she slept. "I should throw you out of the house right now." Her words came out scratchy, making her throat hurt.

Mr. Kitty chuffed, gave her an "as if" look, and then sprang off her chest onto the floor. She swore the force of his jump was strong enough to leave bruises on her. She sat up, prepared to fling curses at him, and then realized she wasn't in her bed, but on the couch instead.

She must have fallen asleep there after sharing Cora's grief. Memories of the previous night flooded her throbbing head...crying, laughing, too much of Clarabelle's relaxation tea, and her thoughts left her in a panic.

Cora?

Hazel quickly scanned her living room and would have missed Cora lying on the floor on the opposite side of the coffee table if not for catching a glimpse of her toes peeking out from the end.

At least her friend hadn't wandered out into the night alone with Hazel passed out on the couch.

But still, she'd let a grieving friend crash on the floor? What kind of hostess was she?

She stood and winced at the piercing pain that slid through her temples like a hot steel rod. A wave of nausea rolled through her, and she quickly covered her mouth.

After a moment, the feeling passed, and she could breathe easier. She peeked over the table, finding Cora wrapped like a burrito in one of her grandmother's quilts. The woman lay on her back, her mouth open, releasing soft snores with each breath.

If Hazel didn't know better, she'd think they'd indulged in too many bottles of wine the previous night, but all they'd had was tea.

Clarabelle's tea. She narrowed her eyes and shook her head. The stuff had obviously been more potent than she'd expected. If grief wasn't enough for Cora, Hazel had practically poisoned her, too.

But it made no sense. The ingredients she'd used were all benign, simple herbs. They couldn't affect her and Cora in such a way.

It must have been the spell she'd cast along with it. She must have said a wrong word, or said it in the wrong way, or...

Blessed Mother help her.

With tender, careful steps, she made her way around the end of the coffee table and lowered her hand toward Cora's shoulder to give her a soft shake. The second her fingers touched her friend, a shrill meow pierced the air. She cried out in surprise and turned fast enough toward Mr. Kitty that she banged her shin into the coffee table.

"Son of a crunchy biscuit," she ground out between clenched teeth,

Hazel pointed an accusing finger at her cat. "I swear, one day..."

She left the threat to hang in the air between them.

Mr. Kitty caterwauled again before launching himself up on the mantel where he proceeded to tip her small clock onto the carpeted floor.

This time, Hazel growled, ignored the throbbing pain in her head, and barreled toward him. "You little rascal." She reached down to grab him, and he dashed between her legs, a flash of ginger fur and then gone.

She grumbled beneath her breath and bent to pick up the clock. When she straightened, the room tilted, and she was forced to grab the mantel to keep from tipping over.

She felt like three-day-old turkey dung. Maybe she was getting sick.

She filled her lungs and then lifted the clock to set it on the mantel. As she did, she glanced at the clock's face, and then her heart jumped up to choke her.

Nine-forty-five? Holy harpies.

She'd overslept by more than three hours. Gretta would be arriving at her shop any minute, the same shop that should be opening in only fifteen. Even if she rushed through her morning routine, she wouldn't make it on time.

Mr. Kitty gave her a sassy meow as he strutted in front of her.

She drew her brows into a frown and then a curious thought hit. "Were you trying to wake me up? So that I wouldn't be late?"

He released a string of meows before he flashed his back end toward her and trotted from the room.

Hazel knew when someone had given her a piece of his mind, and that's exactly what this felt like. "I'm sorry," she called after him, feeling worse than ever.

She'd have to make it up to him. Cook them salmon for dinner, maybe. Then again, maybe he hadn't woken her for her sake. Maybe he'd only wanted his breakfast.

A low groan rumbled from the snuggled burrito lying on her floor, and Hazel shifted her gaze to Cora. "Yeah. That's exactly how I feel, too," she whispered.

She needed to call Gretta to see if she could cover the teashop this morning. Thank heavens she'd asked Lobster Lucy the night before to come in for the day for Cora, too. Neither one of them were fit for work.

Even if Cora felt like going in at some point, she'd need backup. She wasn't in any shape to manage a bustling café.

Hazel searched for her phone and found it beneath one of the couch cushions where it must have slipped during the night. Gretta sounded far too perky when she answered the phone.

"Hey," Hazel said in greeting, her voice sounding like she'd drank gravel the night before.

"Where are you?" Gretta fired off, ignoring their usual pleasantries. "Is everything okay?"

"Yeah. I'm fine. I stayed up late with Cora and must not have heard my alarm." Probably because her phone had been buried in the couch. "Can you cover for a few hours this morning?"

A snort of humor came across the line. "You know I can."

The reprieve lifted a huge weight from her chest, and Hazel was ever-so-grateful she'd found her terrific assistant. "Thanks."

Hazel expected Gretta to sign off and hang up, but only silence came across the line for several long seconds. Then a sigh. "If Cora was with you, then I guess you know what happened."

Hazel glanced toward her sleeping friend and stepped into the kitchen. "I know." She spoke softly. "I was there when they fished Belinda out."

"Seriously?" Gretta's voice was a mixture of concern and interest. "Do you know what happened to her?"

"No more than you do. I left shortly after, and I've been with Cora ever since." She'd hoped to get a call from Peter at some point last evening, but nothing.

"Well...that's good. I'm glad you're with her. Belinda was a pain in my pachootsky, but I know Cora liked her. Don't worry about the shop. I'll cover all day if you need me to. Just take care of Cora. She doesn't have family, so she'll need someone."

Hazel wondered if Peter had managed to contact Belinda's family, wherever they were, if she even had any living, to notify them of her death. "Thanks, Gretta. If I haven't told you before, I appreciate you so much."

A soft chuckle came across the phone. "You'd do the same for me."

She would, Hazel realized. She didn't have family in Stonebridge, either, but these people had filled that spot. "Of course, I would."

Hazel promised to check in with Gretta in a while, and then she ended the call. Back in the living room, Cora was snoring again, and a big part of Hazel's heart begged her to leave Cora alone and let her sleep.

But she couldn't. A new day had come, and Cora had to face it. Though Hazel would make sure she didn't do it alone.

She knelt next to her friend and gave her shoulder a gentle shake. Cora blinked, muttered, and then closed her eyes again.

Hazel tried again, and this time Cora focused on her with the red, swollen eyes of someone grief-stricken.

"Hi there." Hazel smiled and swallowed past the pain in her throat. She must be getting sick. That would explain so much. "How are you?"

"Head hurts." Cora's voice sounded a lot like Hazel's and she realized she'd have to chalk it up to her bad spell-casting skills.

She did her best to bury her pride. For a witch who boasted about making excellent tea, the thought that she'd screwed that up didn't set well with her. "I'm sorry. Mine hurts, too. I must have done something wrong when making tea last night."

Cora glanced about the room as though trying to get her bearings. "Yeah, I think so, too."

Great. "I'm sorry I let you sleep on the floor when there was a perfectly good bed available. I don't even remember falling asleep."

Cora shifted to a sitting position and groaned. "I don't remember much either. Just that I woke up sometime during the night and was cold. I found this quilt on the back of the couch and wrapped up in it, and that's the last thing I remember."

She really was the worst friend. "You should have woken me up."

Her friend attempted a snort and then stopped, placing two fingers against her right temple. "Grabbing the blanket was all I could muster. Blessed Mother, I feel like I've been on a two-day bender."

"Same. If you think you can manage your way to the kitchen, I'll brew us up something for the headaches."

"Only if you promise not to drug me again."

She winced. She supposed she deserved that. "I promise. This one will be a tried and true recipe, not an untested, old family one."

"Ah. One of those. I think things were much different back then. Got to be careful with the old ones. That or your magic is a lot stronger than the person who crafted the potion."

Hazel rolled her eyes. "Doubt that." Clarabelle's powers and potions were obviously much stronger than hers.

A few minutes later, they were both seated at the kitchen table with steaming mugs between their hands. They spoke little as they sipped and allowed Hazel's tea to work its magic. By degrees, the pain and pounding in Hazel's head eased.

Cora sighed. "I think I might actually survive. At least I feel like I got a good night's sleep, and I probably wouldn't have otherwise."

"Yeah. Same. Yesterday was an awful day."

"The worst."

Hazel eyed her friend, wondering if she was up for this conversation. "Are you feeling any better today?"

"Not really. I still can't believe she's gone. She had so much potential, but she just couldn't see it."

Hazel hadn't seen that side of Belinda, but Cora knew her much better.

Cora's gaze drifted to somewhere else for a moment and then she blinked away the moisture accumulating in her eyes. "She struggled to get along with the group, though. Said they didn't understand her. As within any system, there is a hierarchy, and she balked at it. She didn't trust most of the others, and she wouldn't listen to what they had to say."

Hazel remembered the sloppy inverted pentagram that had been drawn on Belinda's arm. "You make it sound like one of your group might have had a vendetta against her. Did they dislike each other enough for one of them to drown her?"

"No," she answered quickly. "None of them would take it that far. They might curse her and make it so she couldn't use her glamour or some such thing, but I think all of us in town realize that we need each other. Besides, when I checked my phone a few minutes ago, several of the coven had messaged me saying witnesses at the lake said she was alone and acting very drunk."

But that didn't explain the pentagram.

Hazel battled her conscience, trying to decide if she should tell Cora. She had to. Cora had become like a sister to her, and if something nefarious had happened to Belinda, she couldn't ignore it.

"Cora?" She met and held her friend's gaze. "When I was at the lake yesterday, I saw something. On Belinda. It looked as though someone had used a thick marker and drawn an inverted pentagram on the underneath of her bicep. Does that sound like something Belinda would do to herself? An act of rebellion maybe?"

Cora stared at her for a long, hard moment, and then slowly shook her head. "No. I know Belinda was headstrong and did have a rebellious streak, but she believed wholeheartedly in the traditions and strength of our craft. I can't picture her dishonoring it in any way. That was one of the things I admired about her."

"I wonder, too, about her drowning. You said she was an excellent swimmer. She would have to have been pretty drunk to not be able to make it back to shore."

Cora blinked several times and studied Hazel. "Are you saying you don't think her death was an accident?"

Hazel traced the handle on her mug. "All I'm saying is there are things that don't seem to add up. The pentagram, for one. Most people think an inverted pentagram is the sign of the devil, but we know otherwise. You don't think Belinda would do that to herself, so I can't help but wonder who would. Peter told me when we first met that if someone in Stonebridge was suspected of being a witch and they stuck around town, they might likely disappear."

Cora nodded thoughtfully. "I've heard rumors of that from years ago, but I don't think anything has happened recently. At least not that I know of."

"But let's say that Belinda managed to somehow reveal herself to one of those who play for the haters. I worry they may have done something about it."

She lifted her tea and sipped. "If we're going to consider murder as a possibility, then we should look at Quentin, too. I can't see him killing anyone, but he was furious with Belinda the other day."

"Yes." Hazel stood and retrieved a pad of paper and pen from a nearby drawer, and then returned to the table. The yellow legal pad reminded her of Peter when he took notes, and her heart smiled.

She wrote Timothy Franklin as well as Samuel Canterbury, the guys who she knew to be witch-haters, on one line, and then Quentin's name below theirs. "What about Charlie? He wasn't too happy about being dumped."

Cora shook her head. "Charlie is such a good guy. I can't picture him doing something like that."

"Sometimes people are very good at hiding their true selves. Look at us. No one in town would suspect us of being witches."

She glanced between the notepad and Hazel, obviously not happy about adding Charlie. "I guess that's true. I just hate to think that someone who comes into my café often could be capable of murder."

Hazel compressed her lips and tapped the pen against the pad of paper. "I don't like considering that either, but I don't think we should rule him out. Anyone else who might not like Belinda?"

Cora gnawed on her bottom lip for several moments. "I guess if we're going to consider everyone, we should add Glenys Everwood to the list. Rumor was that Belinda was trying to steal her boyfriend."

Something in Cora's eyes or perhaps an emotion radiating from her tipped off Hazel. "She's a witch, isn't she?"

Cora paused and then nodded, guilt coloring her features. "I shouldn't tell you. She hasn't given her permission. But I can trust you, right? You'd never do anything to hurt one of us?"

Hazel reached across the table and grasped one of Cora's hands. "Of course not. Never. You know me better than that."

The tension in the room eased. "I think I do, Hazel. I've seen into your heart, and it's a good one."

Her words tugged at Hazel. "I feel the same about you, Cora. You're the sister I never had."

Tears sprang to Cora's eyes. Hazel realized Cora might have felt that way about Belinda, too, and she quickly shook her head. "I'm so sorry. I didn't mean to make you cry again. You've had too much of that."

Cora sniffed. "It's okay. Tears cleanse us."

Hazel agreed with a kind smile. "So, now that we have all these questions, we need to figure out what to do with them, and how to get answers."

"You can talk to Peter. He'll listen to you."

He'd listen, all right, but she wasn't sure what she could reveal to him without exposing herself. "I don't think I can talk to him about the pentagram. I'm sure he's seen it by now, but I didn't say anything yesterday. If I tell him the true meaning behind it, I don't want him to question why I know about such things."

Cora nodded in understanding. "But you could mention that she's a good swimmer, right? And you could tell him that, as long as I've known her, she hasn't been one to drink much."

Yes, that would be a good start. "I'll try to talk to him today. In the meantime, how about if I cook us some breakfast? It won't be anywhere near as good as your food, but I'm sure I can manage something."

Gratitude washed over Cora's face. "You don't know how wonderful that sounds. I'm always expected to be the cook and take care of others, so it's nice to have someone fret over me."

Hazel smiled, stood, and headed to the fridge to gather ingredients. If Peter didn't call her by lunch time, she'd find a reason to visit him at the station. She knew he was busy, but he couldn't expect her to wait forever for answers.

CHAPTER TEN

A misty morning hung over Stonebridge when Hazel dropped Cora at her house just before noon. Since she hadn't heard from Peter, Hazel turned her car toward the police station, but a moment later, her phone rang. She glanced at the screen and smiled. The man must have read her mind.

With a push on her brakes, she pulled to the side of the road, parking her Honda within view of the Old Stone Church. She pushed the answer button on her phone and shifted her gaze back to the church to study its incredible architecture. "Hello?"

"Hazel?" Peter's voice came across the phone smooth and sexy. "Sorry I haven't called. It's been crazy around here."

She wanted to say no worries, but she had worried and wondered. "At least I'm talking to you now. How are things?"

He released a long sigh. "Messy."

She drew her brows together. "That doesn't sound good."

"It isn't. Hey, I was wondering if you could slip away from the shop and meet me. I've already lost my cool with the guys this morning, and I need a few minutes away."

Exactly what she'd been hoping for. "Of course. I actually haven't been into my shop yet this morning. I just dropped off Cora, and I'm sitting in front of the old church."

"Great. Wait for me. I'll be there in two." He hung up before she could reply.

It seemed only moments before Peter pulled up behind her car. He exited, and she did, too. He strode forward, placed his hands on her upper arms, and kissed her on the lips. "Thanks for coming, Hazel."

She blinked in surprise. "Of course." Had they reached the point that they were that familiar with each other? She weighed the idea. They did like each other, and it seemed they trusted each other...with most things.

So, yeah, maybe they had progressed that far. In any other town, she would already be calling Peter her boyfriend.

He took her hand and led her across the street to where a paved path wandered through one of the town's beautiful parks. Fat robins tweeted from their perches high in the trees. In the gardens all around them, red tulips and sunny daffodils vibrated with life.

The Blessed Mother's glorious beauty, showcased at its finest.

She lifted her gaze to Peter and studied the hard lines of his jaw. "You seem pretty stressed."

He blew out a frustrated breath. "You have no idea."

That would be because he hadn't told her a thing. She squeezed his hand and took some of his anxiety as her own. "Is it all from Belinda's case, or something else, too?"

"It's all the investigation. People are saying suicide. Others call it an accidental drowning. Still more claiming she was a witch who deserved to be murdered." He paused to fill his lungs. "Most of the evidence is compromised at best and not giving us many clues."

Her train of thought derailed at the mention of witch. "A witch? Why would they say that?"

Peter flicked his gaze from her and focused on the duck pond up ahead. She had the distinct impression he was holding back, and that thought bothered her. If she had to guess, she'd say the inverted pentagram was at play on the authorities' minds as well.

Finally, he scrubbed the day-old scruff on his chin and sighed. "I don't know. That's what they always say."

She drew her brows together. "But you're acting like you believe them. What if it has nothing to do with witchcraft?"

He snorted and smiled at her as though she was a child. "Trust me, Hazel. We're following all leads and possibilities."

She stiffened as though he'd schooled her. "I'm sure you are."

He lifted a thumb and traced it down her cheek. "Please don't be angry that you can't be involved this time."

She frowned, not happy that he'd read her so easily. "I'm not a petulant child who's mad because I can't go to the zoo with the other kids. I can't help it if I'm interested."

He opened his palms in a show of defeat. "I know. I know. I didn't mean to insinuate that."

Hazel inhaled blossom-scented air and let it cleanse her irritation. Then she sifted through what he'd said. "Has the coroner determined she was alive when she went into the water?" She knew enough about police procedures to know they could determine that sort of thing.

This time, he didn't hesitate to answer. "Yes, the coroner said she was still alive. He estimated she'd been there about eleven hours which would place her time of death around one in the morning. We don't know whether she was conscious or not."

They stopped at the center of the stone footbridge and leaned on the wall to watch the stream amble past. "I guess that still doesn't tell you much other than she wasn't murdered somewhere else and dumped in the pond."

"Exactly." He shifted to face her, and she took in the dark circles under his eyes and the desperation emanating from him.

His need tugged at her heart. She shifted so that she faced him squarely and wrapped her fingers around his arm near his elbow. "I'm so sorry."

He relaxed slightly. "To make matters worse, apparently Belinda is the niece of a New Jersey state senator, and he's pulling some strings. He's insisting federal agents also investigate, hinting that I don't know how to do my job. And while I wouldn't mind the use of their lab, my men and I are fully competent."

People with egos could be such jerks. "If there's anything I can do to help..."

He stared at her for a long moment. Tingles erupted on her skin, and without warning, he slid a hand around her waist and pulled her tight against him. His mouth covered hers in a heated kiss.

Her heart thundered harder because they were in broad daylight. Part of her wondered if she should stop him before someone saw and started gossiping about the hot kiss between the teashop owner and the police chief. But he pulled away as abruptly as he'd kissed her.

Peter exhaled. "Thanks. I needed that."

She chuckled at how he'd caught her off guard and how quickly he'd made his move. "I actually meant something more along the lines of helping you solve the case, but I'm not complaining."

He kissed her once more lightly on the lips. "I wish I could tell you more about everything, but with the senator breathing down my neck and therefore the mayor, I shouldn't really talk about it."

She frowned. She understood there was a code of conduct he needed to adhere to and that perhaps he shouldn't talk to her about cases like he'd done in the past, but it wasn't as if she was a reporter or someone untrustworthy who might compromise the evidence.

He searched her eyes, his full of concern. "I hope you can understand."

Disappointment and sadness curled into a tight ball inside her. "Of course." She'd likely go insane from wonder, but she had no choice.

He wrapped strong arms around her and held her tight against his chest, so tight she could feel his heart beat. "Thanks. Your moral support helps."

Although disappointed, she knew this wasn't all about her, and she did want to help him, not just solve the case, but in everyday life, too. She stood on her tiptoes, placed a hand on his scruffy cheek, and kissed his tantalizing lips once more. She pulled back, and he smiled. "You can call me whenever you need me."

"I knew there was a reason I liked you." He glanced down the path where they'd come from. "I should get back. Lots of stuff to manage. I just needed a break."

She nodded in agreement and took his hand, and together, they walked back to their vehicles. He helped her into her car before he climbed into his and sped off.

She sighed. She did understand why he couldn't talk to her, but that didn't make it any easier. She certainly didn't want him to jeopardize his career for a relationship that could never last. So, she vowed to help him however she could and try to be happy with that.

She put her car in gear and had driven half a block away from the old church before she realized that although he couldn't share information with her, that didn't mean she couldn't poke around on her own.

In a small parking lot near her teashop, Hazel parked her car. She pulled out her phone and searched for Charlie Rossler's number. She'd first met him when she'd called his landscaping business for help clearing tree limbs from her yard after Stonebridge's epic storm had ripped through her trees.

It just so happened she'd been needing to do some heavy-duty spring cleaning in her yard, plus she'd already received permission from her landlords to put in another small herb garden.

She certainly could do the work on her own, but it would be nice to have help from a landscaper.

If she happened to learn anything from Belinda's ex–boyfriend, that would only be a bonus.

CHAPTER ELEVEN

Hazel woke early on Saturday, happy to have the morning off. Today was the day Charlie was scheduled to help with her yard, and her mind raced with possible ways to mine information about Belinda from him.

Gretta would cover the teashop until late afternoon, and then Hazel would take over. Now that the weather was warmer, her number of customers had increased, and like many shops in town, she stayed open later to accommodate them. She and Gretta split the day, which gave Hazel a chance to tackle her ever-growing to-do list, and Gretta time to play in the evening.

The first tick mark was her weekly shopping at the grocery store. She managed that in record time and then headed home. When she arrived at the house, Mr. Kitty was nowhere to be found, and she wondered if he'd somehow managed to sneak out again. One of these days, she was going to figure out how he did that.

She rushed through her cleaning chores, and then just before noon, she threw together a ham and swiss sandwich, tossed some carrot sticks on the plate so she could say she was being healthy, and then added a lovely dill pickle as a treat. She carried her plate and a glass of lemon water to the table. When she slid out the chair to sit, she discovered Clarabelle's spell book waiting for her. Again.

She wished she could say she was surprised. It seemed every time she turned around the last couple of days, she found the tome waiting for her. Mr. Kitty had memorized her routine and left it in places where he knew she'd have a moment to read it.

Though she had to say leaving it in the fridge was pushing things a little too far. She also wondered if that meant he thought she went looking for snacks too often.

She lifted the book of spells, placed it on the table near her lunch, and sat. With half the sandwich in one hand, she took a bite, and then opened the ancient tome to the kid's bookmark she'd used to mark her spot. With nearly fifty potions and spells listed—yes, she'd counted them all the previous night when she couldn't sleep—she wondered if she would ever remember them, let alone become prolific at using them. Her track record wasn't so good, so far.

She flipped through a couple of the pages in the middle of the book, half noting the ingredients and words she would need to create a potion for wards or to cast a spell to make it rain. A page later, though, an interesting heading jumped out at her.

Clarabelle's truth-telling spell.

Hazel leaned closer and read over the list of necessary ingredients. This was something that could certainly come in handy. She couldn't imagine Peter would disagree with her. Although, he would have to accept witchcraft into his life if he truly were to benefit from it.

Then again, maybe she could find a way to use it and then help Peter with his work. He wouldn't be able to ignore her usefulness then.

A crazy thought entered her mind. Maybe she could use it on Charlie when he showed up that very morning to help her with yard work. She could casually chat him up, and he'd happily volunteer information.

If she learned something valuable to Peter's investigation, she would share with him. She didn't need to explain how she'd made

Charlie talk. If nothing came from it, she didn't need to say a word about her clandestine activities.

Milk from a cow. Two drops of vinegar. Spoon of sugar.

Whether truth be sweet or sour, let it pour from thy mouth this very hour. I call upon the powers that be, bring forth the words, so mote it be.

The first thought that came into her mind was that this was such a simple potion, even the most novice of witches should be able to manage it. Then a quiet but snarky voice reminded her that the eyelash spell she'd tried had also seemed easy, but she'd ended up with purple irises in her eyes instead.

However, in her favor, she was pretty sure the money spell she'd tried had worked. Like, who couldn't use an extra five bucks, right?

She sighed in defeat. There was no way she could attempt that spell on Charlie. Not without testing it first. Cora would probably be a willing test bunny, but if she waited until she had a chance to practice on her friend, she'd miss her opportunity with Charlie. She might get another. Then again, she might not.

She tilted her head as another idea popped into mind. She could give it a quick test drive on herself. She'd buried a few memories, had a few regrets in her lifetime that she didn't necessarily want to be truthful about, but they weren't anything she couldn't manage if they came up. In fact, if she asked herself about them while under this spell, then she would be forced to tell the truth to herself, and the answers she received might help her with unresolved matters from the past.

She glanced at the clock. Charlie wouldn't arrive for another ninety minutes. That should give her plenty of time for a quick experiment.

In her bedroom, she pulled her large suitcase from the closet and plopped it on her bed. She unzipped the lid, opened it, and then felt along the inside until her fingers ran across the small indent that would allow her to pull open the false bottom. She'd been careful not to bring too many items that might expose her as a witch, but there were some things that a lady couldn't do without. Especially if they were items she'd be unable to get in Stonebridge.

Such as an object of protection. With her track record, she thought it best to be safe rather than sorry.

She opened a small pouch and pulled her black tourmaline necklace from inside. The chain was long, allowing it to slip over her head and let the crystal fall beneath her shirt and snuggle between her breasts close to her heart, where it also wouldn't be seen.

She then pulled a small notebook from her nightstand and spent a few moments pondering what aspects of her life would be worth digging into to have answers. The first to surface was her previous, complicated relationship with Victor.

He'd been her first real love, and though she'd convinced herself she was over him and the damage he'd done to her by cheating, she'd like to know for sure if the sting she still felt every time she thought of him was residue or the result of her still trying to process his betrayal.

Did she truly believe she could forever be safe in Stonebridge?

She added a fun question about whether she'd rather be thinner or eat more cherry macaroons.

Finally, she acknowledged the haunting question that had been hovering at the edges of her mind for a while now. Would she ever consider trying one of Clarabelle's dark spells? If necessary, she added.

Satisfied with her questions, she headed to the kitchen and stirred together the truth-telling concoction, going easy on the vinegar, which she felt must be tied to negative truths, just in case Cora had been right about things being more potent in earlier times.

Determined to learn the boundaries of the spell, she downed the contents, whispered the words, and waited.

A tingly feeling hummed low in her chest and radiated its vibrations outward. The power of it left her nervous, and she inhaled to calm the sensation, but it remained.

Blessed Mother, she hoped that was a normal reaction. In a way, it made sense. Many things in her world had consequences, good or bad. She believed it was how the Blessed Mother kept balance among living things.

A spell that caused vulnerability by making a person unable to hide her feelings was balanced by the fact that person would be able to detect the magic that caused it. Those natural boundaries protected everyone. Though she doubted anyone outside the magical world would know she'd been drugged.

Hazel relaxed into the feeling and reminded herself to breathe. Witchcraft was in her blood, and she needn't be afraid of it. If she'd lived back in Clarabelle's time, this would probably be a spell she would have tried on her friends like Truth or Dare.

From the corner of her eye, she caught a hint of ginger, and she turned her gaze to find Mr. Kitty watching her from the doorway. His body was taut and alert, and she was certain that he'd sensed her magic and had come to spectate.

However, she was not going to do this in front of him. It might seem silly, but there were some things she wanted to keep private. Especially if she totally screwed it up.

She crossed the kitchen and paused next to him. "Sorry. This one is for me only." She continued to her bedroom, glanced back to find him not far behind, and closed the door in his face.

He wouldn't like it, and she took a moment to appreciate that fact. Too bad for him. She didn't feel obliged to share her magic with him. The cat was far too sassy for his own good, and she didn't need him mocking her if she made a fool of herself.

She just hoped he wouldn't be able to magically walk through a door like she wondered if he could sometimes.

She crawled onto the soft pink patchwork quilt that covered her bed, another heirloom from her seamstress master grandmother. She'd wanted to save this one, but her grandmother had insisted she'd made it to be used, and she would be sad if Hazel locked it away somewhere.

She'd learned never to argue with her grandmother.

Hazel crossed her legs beneath her and leaned back against the pillow. This experiment was harmless, she reminded herself, and she then lifted the notebook with her questions from her nightstand.

She hesitated to read them. Now that she was faced with answering some difficult questions, she wasn't so sure this had been a good idea. Not everyone was meant to be completely honest with themselves, either. Not when memories and thoughts had been put into place to protect hearts and minds.

But if she didn't go through with it, she wouldn't know before Charlie arrived if it worked, logic argued. That had been the point of trying the spell in the first place.

After expelling a deep breath, she skipped the first question about Victor and focused on the next. Did she believe that she was safe staying in Stonebridge like she had convinced herself she was?

No. The answer came immediately and with enough force that it stole her breath. She took a moment to calm down.

Okay. She'd known there was an inherent risk by being here, but one she could mitigate.

Another wave of doubt rolled over her, drawing her anger. Fine. It was dangerous. But this was a risk she wanted to take.

Yes. A sense of peace washed over her, and she knew she'd discovered the depth of that question and could be okay with it.

Holy harpies, she realized. Her spell *had* worked. Clarabelle and Mr. Kitty would be proud.

Onto a harder question. She'd convinced herself that she knew she was over Victor. He'd broken her heart, but she'd pieced it back together, and it was as good as new.

No.

She growled, growing frustrated by the answers. She *was* over him. She had to be.

No.

"Yes," she argued. She'd moved on. In fact, she had a new man in her life. She had no room left in her heart for the one who'd decimated it.

Wrong.

She slammed the notebook closed, tossed it on the bottom of her bed, and stood. Enough of this. Obviously, the spell worked. Continuing further torture wouldn't prove that to her any more than she already knew, and there was no sense ripping open old wounds to prove her point.

She already knew she'd choose cherry macaroons every time, and she didn't want to know what she thought about using Clarabelle's dark spells.

Yes, you do.

Her mind began to explore that question, but the sound of a car door slamming distracted her. She peeked out her bedroom window and found a green truck parked along the curb. A Rossler Landscaping Services logo covered the driver's door, and Hazel muttered a quick prayer of thanks that Charlie had saved her from herself.

CHAPTER TWELVE

Charlie arrived ten minutes early. Hazel wished she'd had a few minutes to chill after her unpleasant question and answer session, but his interruption was well-timed, and she couldn't complain.

She hurried to the living room and secretly watched Charlie stride to her front door. His gait was long and sure, and his faded red t-shirt outlined his muscled torso, encouraging a moment of appreciation from her. Not that he was her type or anything, but he was cute. Her conscience immediately slapped back with a reminder that he might be her type. She cursed her bad luck.

He knocked. She crossed to the front door and opened it with a smile. "Good morning."

Charlie dipped his head in greeting. "Morning Hazel. Ready for me to get started?" He seemed to be in a good mood, and she wondered if that meant something. Perhaps he was happier now that Belinda was no longer on earth. Maybe he'd finally realized he was better off without her in his life. Regardless, he didn't seem too brokenhearted.

"You're a little early." Stunned at the words tumbling from her mouth, she clamped her lips shut and realization settled over her. The spell would work for anyone who talked to her until it wore off. Anyone...with any questions.

A frown settled across his forehead. He pulled the phone from his pocket and checked the time. "Ten minutes." He shrugged. "I can wait in my truck if you'd like."

She wanted to tell him that she'd meant to say ten minutes early was great, but the words wouldn't come. *Holy harpies.*

It took her several seconds to process what her mouth could speak. "No, no. Now will be just fine. I'm so happy to have you here."

The smile returned to his face. "Great. I appreciate the work."

"Of course. I know what it's like to be a small business owner. There's no guaranteed paycheck if we don't work."

He dipped his head in agreement. "Yes, ma'am."

She needed a minute to compose herself. "I think we should start with trimming up the trees. Let me grab my shoes, and I'll meet you out back and show you where."

"Sounds great." He nodded and turned away.

She closed the door and sagged against it. She really needed to start thinking smarter if she was going to cast any more spells. As it stood, she didn't dare try the truth spell on Charlie until she'd done more research.

Earlier when she'd thought it had been a great idea, she'd only considered its use for answers she wanted to know. Now she could see that it would require her to be honest in every statement that she made. She wasn't sure she could put an innocent person in that situation.

Blessed Mother, she hoped it was a short-lived spell.

When she stepped outside a few moments later, Charlie already had the chainsaw going. He trimmed off the low hanging branches on her biggest red oak tree.

He hadn't noticed her, so she paused and took the opportunity to study him. She opened her senses and searched for hints of malice or the residue that sometimes remained with a person after they'd harmed another. Most people could recognize this kind of underlying blemish in others, and they tended naturally to avoid such people. Still, many didn't understand where the negativity came from like she did.

But she sensed no such darkness in Charlie. In fact, he seemed to have an open and warm heart. Not to mention, a really nice set of biceps.

He twisted, angling toward another limb, and the action pulled his shirt tight across his abs. *Nice.*

Hazel had seen the man Belinda had dumped Charlie for, and she hadn't gotten the best vibe from Grant Weiland. Not to mention, he wasn't much too look at. Especially not compared to Charlie.

The fact that Belinda had chosen Grant over him made her wonder at the poor woman's sanity. Charlie seemed to be a decent, likable fellow, and boy, did he have the looks.

She couldn't say the same about Grant. Though his family did have money, and after hearing what Quentin Fletcher had said about Belinda basically stealing from his grandpa, Hazel would have to guess that money had played an important role in Belinda's life. If her uncle was a state senator, then chances were likely her parents had money as well.

Even so, it hadn't seemed like they'd shared much of it with Belinda. Maybe that's what made her so desperate where money was concerned.

The sound of the chainsaw died to a low growl. A branched cracked, fell to the ground, and bounced on the soft green grass. Charlie must have caught sight of her because he shifted a quick glance in her direction. The smile that followed could have melted even the oldest nun's heart.

He lifted a hand in greeting. "Hey."

She stepped forward, moving until there was only a few feet between them. "Look at you. You're already hard at work."

He shrugged and grinned. "I always aim to please."

"Yes, I can see that you do." She smiled as though she was innocent of any innuendo and then pinned her tongue between her teeth until the need to speak passed.

Focus on the work. That was the only thing that might save her self-respect and reputation.

She glanced about her yard and pointed out various things that she needed help with. "It looks like you know what you're doing with trimming the trees, so I'll leave that to your expertise. Afterward, the shrubs could really use cleaning up. My landlord said I could add another garden, too. I was thinking I'd put it along the north fence so that it gets lots of sunny, southern exposure.

"I don't know what kind of tools you have." She internally groaned at her choice of words. "I mean equipment." She should really stop now.

She sensed him fighting to repress his laughter, and she died inside. "I have whatever you need, Hazel." His low, masculine words hovered in the air between them.

Blessed Mother. Heat flared across her cheeks. Great. Now, he thought she was flirting with him. "I didn't mean…"

He held up a hand, stopping her and chuckled. "It's okay. I know what you meant. Besides, you and Peter are dating, so I probably shouldn't make a play for his girl. It's never a good idea to piss off the cops, and I doubt I'm your type."

"That's not true." The words were out before she could stop them. *No, no, no, no.*

Her answer generated interest in his eyes. "What's not true? You and Peter aren't dating?"

The hole she'd dug grew deeper, but she knew if she tried to clarify her statement, she'd likely be swallowed whole by it.

"We are." She fisted her hands, forcing her nails into the fleshy part of her palms, hoping the pain would shut her up.

Confusion painted his expression. "Then...you want to date us both?"

"No. Never mind. We've gotten way off track." Blessed Mother, she was a mess. She forced a chuckle, hoping to laugh off the situation. "How about while you're busy with the trees, I'll go work in my herb garden. If you have questions, let me know. When you're ready, I'll show you where I want the new garden."

With her cheeks burning, she strode away as fast as her feet would carry her.

Charlie approached her a half hour later, startling her from her thoughts. "Hey."

She looked up from where she'd been clearing grass from around her lavender. She lifted a hand to shade her eyes from the bright sun. "Oh, hey." She wanted to say something funny or lighthearted but didn't trust her mouth.

"All done over there. Do you want to show me where you want the new garden and the approximate dimensions?"

"Sure." She stood, brushed grass from her jeans, and led the way to the area on the north side of the lawn. She buried the end of a shovel approximately five feet from the wooden fence and then counted out paces to equal another ten for the length of it. "Something like this. Doesn't have to be exact."

He nodded and then drove a small wooden spike into the ground near the shovel. He staked out two other corners and ran a length of twine to mark all but one side.

She waited while he retrieved a tiller from his truck and then watched him work the machine, rolling clods of grass deep into the ground while bringing up rich, dark-brown soil. The sight of it stirred her imagination and inspired excitement as she thought of all the things she could grow.

Being an earth witch, she had an affinity for seeds, plants, leaves, and flowers. So many possibilities to create beauty, tea and other potions.

As far as she was concerned, the earth was the Blessed Mother's greatest gift to them all.

In no time, he had the area turned into a beautiful brown square, an artist's palette, to be sure. "That looks fantastic. Just what I imagined. And you did it so fast."

"Great." He grinned, obviously enjoying her approval. "Are you going to use it to grow more herbs for your teashop?"

"No," she said without thinking. "Mostly for personal use."

Curses. She hoped he didn't delve any deeper, or she'd be spouting all the ways she'd used her herbs for potions and salves to help any number of ailments. In the blink of an eye, he might learn all about her witchy abilities.

He eyed the area and then turned back to her. "That's a lot of herbs for one person."

Sweat trickled between her breasts. "I'll send some to my mom, too." That was the truth.

"If you're looking for a place with good prices on plants, check out Harriett's Nursery. Follow Camden, and you'll find it. If you go, tell her I sent you."

They were back to casual conversation. Perfect. "That's great. Thanks so much."

He cleaned up his tools, and she retrieved money to pay him. When she met him outside by his truck, she was surprised at the cloud of high anxiety surrounding him. He'd been fine all morning.

Charlie finished filling out her receipt, separated the yellow copy and handed it to her. He hesitated longer than he should have, and she braced herself for what might come next. "You knew Belinda, right?"

Dang it. Here was the conversation she'd anticipated, and she cursed the fact she didn't maintain control over her full faculties so that she could exploit it. "I didn't know her very well. Mostly just from seeing her at Cora's."

He nodded, his eyes distant. "I can't believe she's gone."

Hazel's heart sank to his vibration, and she placed a comforting hand on his forearm. "I know. I'm sorry for your loss."

Genuine appreciation flickered in his gaze. "Thank you. Not many people understand that, even though we'd broken up, I still cared for her."

"It's hard to turn off those feelings." She'd experienced similar emotions with Victor. She tested her next words in her mind before speaking them to make sure they would come out correctly. "I'm sure it makes it harder to know that one of the last conversations you had was a fight."

He expelled a deep breath. "Yeah. That's right. I forgot you were there."

"She sounded pretty heartless, if you ask me."

His expression grew sadder, and she cursed herself for her honesty.

"She was mad because I wouldn't agree with her that it was over. I still think we could have made things work. But she'd found someone new. Grant Weiland. Harvard graduate. She always was one to want the newest, shiniest things."

A spark of anger touched his last words. But she couldn't tell if the resentment intertwined with his feelings was enough for him to want to kill her.

If not Charlie, then perhaps Grant was the murderer. She wondered if Peter had checked out Belinda's latest boyfriend. "I don't know Grant very well."

Charlie snorted his derision. "He's as shallow and materialistic as they come. He'd been dating Glenys Everwood but told Belinda he'd broken up with her."

Glenys Everwood again, she noted.

"But a friend told me she'd seen him and Glenys together out by Redemption Pond."

That didn't necessarily mean anything. "Maybe he was letting her down easy."

He tossed the receipt book in the open passenger door of his truck and closed it. "That's not what I heard. The only type of laying was him on top of her, if you know what I mean."

"Oh..." She drew out the word. "I see." That was a problem then. A lover's triangle never ended well for at least one of them.

Anger flashed in his eyes, and his gaze lasered on Hazel. "Belinda was a toy to him, something to be used and tossed. But I couldn't get her to see that."

Her hackles rose in response. Perhaps, she shouldn't have encouraged this conversation.

He gripped his hands into fists and then released them. "She trusted him over me, and now she's dead."

A freezing tendril of fear drew down her back, leaving her with shivers. A Charlie fierce with hatred had replaced the kind one who'd shown up to help her. She couldn't tell, though, if he was angry at Belinda or at who had stolen his possibility of reconciliation.

She needed to steer them back to safer ground. "I'm so sorry, Charlie. I know Peter will find the killer soon. He won't give up until he does."

As quickly as his anger had reared, it disappeared. His shoulders sagged, and sadness permeated everything about him. He shook his head. "Even if he does, it won't bring her back."

She held her gaze steady and kept her tone low and calm. "But it might bring closure, and that could help you."

Emotion welled in his eyes. He drew his knuckles beneath his nose as his openness retreated into darkness. "Thanks for listening, Hazel. Sorry to dump all this on you."

Her heart reached out to him, trying to reconnect. "No, don't be sorry. This is a lot to bear."

He gave one quick nod. "I've gotta go. Thanks again for the work."

"Thank you for your help," she said, but he'd already turned away.

He strode to the driver's side and opened his truck door. He closed it with a slam. The engine started, and Charlie drove away like demons chased him.

Hazel hesitated all of five seconds before she pulled her phone from her pocket and fired off a message to Peter, asking him to stop by her house when he'd finished his day. She wasn't too happy that the flow of information would likely be one-sided during their conversation, but she felt Peter needed what insight she could give him from her interaction with Charlie.

Then she remembered the curse she'd placed upon herself and considered retracting her offer. But, on second thought, she could wait a few hours and see what happened. If the curse remained, she could call off her invitation then.

CHAPTER THIRTEEN

When Hazel received a text from Peter several hours later stating he was on his way, she slipped the bowl of beef stew from the fridge and placed it in the microwave to reheat it. The curse had lifted not long after she'd gone into her shop, and she'd hoped Peter would have been able to leave for the day by dinnertime. With the magnitude of this case, she should have known better.

A knock sounded on her front door, sending her pulse racing. "Why do you have to do that every single time?" she muttered to her body as she strode through her living room.

Mr. Kitty answered her question with a loud meow.

She cast him a sideways glance. "I wasn't talking to you."

When she reached the door, she inhaled deeply, exhaled, and then opened it. "Hey," she said with a smile in her heart. Even if Peter had frustrated her more than usual lately, she was addicted to the delicious feelings that pervaded her every time she peered into those devastating green eyes.

A look of genuine happiness resided in his tired expression. "Hey, beautiful." Without asking, he pulled her into his arms and placed a possessive kiss on her lips.

She soaked up pleasure until he leaned back, leaving her breathless.

"Something smells really good." His stomach rumbled in agreement. "I haven't eaten since breakfast."

"Come on in." She grasped his hand and tugged him toward her kitchen. "Not eating is not smart. How are you going to be at the top of your game if you don't? Then the feds will walk all over you."

"I know. I know. Things have been crazy busy, and I just forgot until I walked in here."

She pushed him into a chair, loving the feel of his strong shoulders beneath her fingertips. "Sit down and let me take care of you. If you're not going to look out for yourself, then someone has to."

He smiled at her in relief, and her heart slipped farther down the slippery slope. "Thank you, Hazel. You're a godsend."

Or sent from the Blessed Mother, she though. Either way, making him happy made her happy.

She dished up rich stew, pulled a spoon from a drawer, and took it to him.

His eyes widened in anticipation. "Homecooked or canned?"

"Homecooked, of course." Though she had used a recipe from Cora.

He groaned in pleasure. "Lord, have mercy on my soul." He lifted a spoonful to his lips and groaned again as he ate his first bite.

She chuckled, enjoying the pleasant sensations that came from giving to another person. "I forgot the rolls." She retrieved the covered plate of sourdough rolls that she'd picked up from Cora's earlier.

He tilted his neck to each side as though stretching his muscles. "Amazing," he said with his mouthful.

She smiled, knowing he was embellishing his praise but enjoying it all the same. "I can't take credit for the rolls."

"Don't care." He spooned in another bite, chewed and swallowed. "It's all excellent."

More than anything, she loved helping people. "I'm glad."

She kept the conversation friendly and casual until he'd finished. "Do you have time to hang out for a while? I wouldn't mind crashing on the couch."

"For you? Anything." He rotated his head as they walked into the living room.

"Neck bothering you?" She didn't need him to answer to know that it was.

He squeezed the back of his neck. "Too many hours at the desk."

The man worked too hard on a regular day in her opinion, but he was dedicated, and she admired him for that. "I have some ointment I made that might help."

"If you're offering a rub, I'll take it. Anything to ease the pain."

She had the perfect cure. "I'll be right back."

She retrieved the small jar of balm she'd concocted out of eucalyptus and ginger and returned to the living room to find a shirtless, far-too-handsome police chief sitting on the edge of her couch with his gun and holster resting on her coffee table. She supposed it was a logical conclusion that he'd need to remove his shirt, but she'd only meant to rub his neck.

He shifted to give her full access to his back.

She tried to pretend she wouldn't enjoy this as much as he would and dipped her fingers into the smooth, scented ointment. She rubbed the concoction between her hands and then spread it from the base of his neck outward.

As her fingers glided over his skin, a shiver enveloped her. She marveled at the strength in his back and the width of his shoulders. Freckles scattered across the tops of his shoulders, likely from exposure to sun.

He dropped his head forward. "That feels amazing."

She drove her thumbs up the center of his neck and then focused pressure just below his skull. "You're a mess."

He snorted in agreement.

She worked the tightly strung trapezius muscles running across the tops of his shoulders, trying to apply enough pressure to relax them without pushing too hard. "Let me know if I hurt you."

"You're fine." He stretched his neck to the side as she worked. "Smells good."

She was rather proud of this blend. All her friends and her mother's friends asked for jars. She'd shared her recipe, but they all complained theirs didn't turn out the same. She was glad Peter liked it, too. "Thanks. It should feel warm on your skin."

"It's definitely working. You have an incredible touch."

She'd also been told that before. She assumed it was part of her healing gifts. "Thank you."

A soft vibrational humming filled her senses, and she enjoyed being in sync with him. Despite their differences, they did share a similar frequency.

She hesitated to bring up Belinda's case because she didn't want to chance ruining their lovely evening, but she had invited him over for a reason. "I know you can't talk much about the case."

He sighed. "I really can't."

She'd already decided not to let that bother her. Even though it did. But she wouldn't hold it against him. "That's fine. I'm not asking for information. I only wanted to share a little of mine."

With his muscles sufficiently warmed and stretched, she removed her hands and rubbed the remaining balm over her forearms. A delicious tingling sank beneath her skin as she sat next to him.

He eyed her with a wary look as he, unfortunately, donned his shirt.

"I mean it. You don't have to share anything." Though she wouldn't mind if he did. "I wanted to let you know I had a conversation today with Charlie Rossler."

He frowned.

She sent him a sweet smile. "Just because you're not telling me anything doesn't mean I can't ask around a little."

"You shouldn't be interfering in the investigation."

She shrugged off the building irritation. "A conversation between fellow townsfolk does not constitute interference. Besides, you know I can't resist asking a few questions."

He rolled his eyes and shook his head. "Yes, I do know this about you."

She grinned. "And you like me anyway."

"Yes. Yes, I do." He lifted expectant brows. "So, tell me already."

Excitement fluttered in her veins. "Charlie was here helping me with some landscaping."

"That sounds convenient. You know you can ask me for help."

She waved off his comment. "You're busy, and I didn't want to bother you."

"Uh-huh."

She knew he'd seen right through her story, but she still wouldn't own it. Even if he wouldn't share what he knew, he couldn't stop her from getting information her way. "He didn't say much about Belinda until he was ready to leave. For a while, I thought maybe he didn't care about her death at all. I guess he was just holding back."

Peter nodded thoughtfully. "He was pretty mellow when we interviewed him, too. Almost too much."

"I think it's because he's hiding his feelings. He mentioned that most people thought he shouldn't care because they'd broken up, but let me tell you, he cares. Even after she dumped him for Grant

Weiland, he still wanted her back. He thought Grant was playing with her on the side while he was still with Glenys."

She drew a strand of hair across her lips while thoughts tumbled freely through her mind. "I feel like maybe Glenys might be more likely to want Belinda out of the picture than Charlie."

He stretched his legs out in front of him and leaned back. "Already interviewed her. She has an alibi."

Hazel's shoulders sagged even as she continued to wade through the details. "Is it a solid alibi?"

"Rock solid. Harriett Palmer said they'd had a girls' night out. Dinner together, and then they'd gone back to Glenys' house where they'd consumed two bottles of wine over the course of the evening. Harriett ended up spending the night in Glenys' spare bedroom because she didn't want to drive."

Her interest deepened. "If Harriett was drunk, then it *could* be possible that Glenys slipped out at some point."

"Harriett didn't think so. She said they were both hammered. Too drunk to drive, let alone pull off that murder."

She still wasn't convinced. "What if—"

"I think you need to consider someone else, Hazel. She's the manager of Stonebridge Bank. A nice-looking lady, if you ask me."

Hazel narrowed her gaze.

He sighed in exasperation. "Let me finish. She says she didn't believe Grant had a relationship with Belinda. That Belinda had flirted with him a few times, but the flirtation was all one-sided, and that their relationship is solid."

"Doesn't mean Grant couldn't have hidden it from her."

Peter reached over, wrapped his fingers around her arm, and tugged her to him. She went willingly. She leaned her back against his chest, and she basked in the pleasure of him snuggling her in an embrace.

He kissed her hair, and she smiled. "Yes, I can't one-hundred-percent rule out Glenys, but it makes no sense for her to kill Belinda. First, Grant's not the type to be interested in a server. He's all about social status, constantly talking about his family's holdings and background. What Glenys has to offer would be more attractive to him."

"Belinda is very pretty."

"Glenys is, too."

"Maybe Glenys isn't very nice. Maybe she's controlling, and Grant didn't like that," she argued though she didn't know why.

He stroked her arm with his thumb, igniting tingles inside her. "I'm not saying we've ruled her out one hundred percent, but she's not at the top of our list."

Hazel nodded in acceptance, though she intended to do a little digging of her own where Glenys was concerned before she completely agreed. "Who is at the top, then? If you can tell me."

"Charlie, for one."

She started to argue, but he cut her off. "We're considering Quentin Fletcher, too. From all accounts, he was livid and threatening the day he yelled at Belinda, and she'd embarrassed him in public on several occasions before that. I haven't ruled out Cora, either."

"*No.*" The word exploded from her mouth. "No way. How could you even consider her?"

He tightened his hold on her. "She's been giving Cora trouble for some time, including the incident with Quentin's grandfather. That's not good for business."

"Yeah, but she could have just fired her."

"Well, she's not anywhere near the top anyway."

"I should hope not." She inhaled a calming breath, not sure why she was getting worked up over this. Cora was innocent. The facts would never prove otherwise, so she needn't worry. And Peter always kept everyone on his list until proven otherwise. "Am I on your list of suspects?"

He chuckled. "Not this time."

"Why not? I have no alibi."

"You're not on the list, Hazel." He kissed her hair, and she fought to keep her thinking straight. "Your hair smells really good, by the way."

She knew what he was doing, trying to distract her, but she wasn't ready to end the murder conversation just yet. "Then what about Grant?"

He sighed. "Haven't ruled him out just yet. But he seems unlikely. Mayor's nephew."

"Which might make him think he can get away with stuff."

"Smart guy," Peter continued as though she hadn't interrupted. "Just out of law school. I'm not saying he didn't use Belinda, but I don't think he'd jeopardize everything to kill her. Not when he could just dump her."

Sounded like Peter was letting him off the hook too easily. "Maybe Belinda threatened to tell Glenys."

"It's possible, but again, we don't have much evidence pointing toward that."

She lifted one of his hands from her midsection and wound her fingers through his. The pads of his fingertips were rougher than hers. His hands were strong and capable, and she wondered about all the many things he'd done with them throughout his life. Shoot a weapon. Wipe tears as he buried his wife. The first time he'd held Hazel's hand. So many experiences, and she wished she could know them all. She felt his heart, but she wanted to know so much more.

"There is something else," Peter finally said, surprising her. "I don't know if you noticed the day we pulled Belinda from the water, but she had an odd pentagram drawn on her arm."

She was glad Peter finally mentioned it, but even now, the reminder of it gave her chills. "I did."

"I shouldn't say anything, but I doubt it will remain confidential, not with the number of people involved in the investigation."

Her heart warmed, knowing he trusted her. "Regardless, I won't repeat anything."

He squeezed her hand. "I love that I can trust you. That's important to me."

"Of course."

"We believe the symbol was possibly placed by witches or devil worshipers."

She stiffened at the implication. "They're not the same thing."

"People around here believe that they are."

She remained silent.

He leaned his head against hers. "Have you ever heard anything from anyone about Belinda being a witch?"

She hesitated to answer, first making sure she had her emotions in check. Good thing she wasn't under the truth spell right now.

She also noticed that, while he trusted her, she couldn't give him the same respect, and ultimately, that would be a problem. "Is that what people are saying?" she asked, avoiding directly answering his question.

"It's been mentioned several times. The pentagram is often used by Satanists."

It burned that she couldn't defend her kind. "I did hear someone mention something about a secret society in town who hunts witches. Maybe they did it and used the mark to brand her."

He snorted. "There's no secret society."

Or at least none that he knew about. Or none that he would admit to.

She sighed, wishing their backgrounds didn't have to be at odds. Despite her ancestral grandmother's approval of Peter, she wondered again if she should have let him into her life. Her heart argued that she should, but her mind was in complete opposition most of the time.

He shifted on the couch until they both had their feet up and she was curled against him in his embrace. "Hey, how about we don't spend all night talking about murder and suspects? I would love to put that out of my mind for a while and focus on you."

Her heart called out a victory, and she let it win for now. She did love spending time with him. Even if their thoughts and ideas weren't in sync, their hearts and bodies were. "What do you want to know?" She hoped it had nothing to do with witchcraft.

She sensed his muscles and mind relaxing and allowed hers to follow.

"Tell me about your childhood. Where you grew up. What your family is like."

"It's not that interesting," she started. This, she could do. She'd tell him about her life with the exception of witchcraft. Afterward, she'd ask him about his. She wanted to know more about the man and loved that he wanted to know her, too.

Maybe if she kept her heart open and had faith in him, she'd discover a way for them to be together. He was a good man, after all.

CHAPTER FOURTEEN

Days later, Peter's insistence that she stay out of the investigation still echoed in Hazel's mind, growing louder with each step she took toward the bank. She understood the importance of letting him do his job. She really did.

But talking with the bank manager about opening a business account was a legitimate reason to enter the building. Her visit didn't necessarily have anything to do with a certain recent crime. She'd needed to separate her personal banking from her business for a while now.

A friendly visit to Stonebridge's bank. No harm. No foul.

She pulled open the glass door and stepped inside. Warm opulence greeted her. Lots of glass and dark woods had been combined with deep forest green accents. A slight woodsy scent clung to the air. That wasn't something she typically found in banks, but she liked the welcoming and comforting feeling it gave her.

Hazel approached a man near her age who sat behind a desk near the entrance. He glanced up at her, deep blue eyes peering through black-rimmed glasses that matched the color of his dark brown hair. "Good morning...Ms. Hardy, correct?"

She found a warm heart behind those gorgeous eyes and widened her smile. "Yes, good morning." She glanced at the name placard on the desk. Lachlan Brogan, Loan Officer.

"Is there something I can help you with today?" His cultured voice and pleasant demeanor was like warm chocolate down a frozen throat. She could use more people like this in her life.

"I need to open a business account. I run my teashop as a sole proprietorship, and I've used my personal account up until now, but I really should separate them."

"Yes, Ms. Hardy. That is always a good idea." He opened a drawer and pulled a form from his desk. "If you want to fill this out, someone will be with you in a minute."

She hoped she could at least catch a glance of Glenys while she was there. "Thank you very much."

"I'll help her," a female voice called. "Sally might be a few minutes."

Hazel shifted her gaze toward the row of teller stations and found a slender woman, very pixie-like except for her height, walking toward them. A lavender blouse set off her dark blue business suit and contrasted beautifully with her short mahogany hair.

The woman extended her hand. "Glenys Everwood, branch manager, at your service."

Peter had been right. Glenys was beautiful.

Hazel shook her hand, remaining friendly though she struggled to pinpoint the woman's aura. "Hazel Hardy of Teas and Temptations just down the street."

Glenys nodded. "That's right. Nice to finally meet you. I've been meaning to stop in for a while now." She gestured with her head to the left. "Let's step into my office, shall we?"

Hazel followed the confident woman into her office where she closed the door and offered Hazel a seat in one of the olive green, tufted back armchairs.

Glenys took a pen from a green glass holder sitting at the corner of her desk and passed it to Hazel. "Should just take you a minute to fill this out."

She smiled at the woman, trying to assess her. "Thanks so much for taking time with me."

Glenys returned an equally sugary smile. "Our customers are like gold to us."

Hazel nodded and turned her attention to the form. Business name. Owner's name. Address.

A sharp pinch nipped at the base of Hazel's skull. "*Ouch.*" The second the words left her mouth, she realized her mistake.

Glenys widened her eyes as though surprised and then narrowed them. "Are you okay?"

Hazel had no idea how to respond to the woman's attempted intrusion into her psyche. "Just...a...yeah. I'm fine." If she called Glenys out for being a witch, she'd give away her identity at the same time. Maybe, for now, it was best to let things be.

A few seconds later, a harder pinch bit her, and Hazel slapped her hand across the back of her neck as though swatting a mosquito. She couldn't let her continue, or she might learn something Hazel didn't want her to. "Something bit me."

"Bit you?" Glenys' smooth voice belied the stark concern in her eyes.

Hazel might not be as cunning and crafty as the witches in Stonebridge had been forced to be, but she did recognize when she'd been probed, thanks to a backstabbing friend in high school.

Unfortunately, Hazel's attempt at a stealthy visit to gain information was about to be as successful as Glenys' prying into her mind. She sighed. "You know very well what's wrong. I'm not an idiot. I can sense when someone is trying to sneak into my thoughts."

Glenys opened her mouth. Closed it. "I can't believe I didn't recognize a sister right off the bat." She shook her head in bewilderment. "You must be the new witch Cora mentioned."

An uncomfortable warning slithered over her. She'd trusted Cora. "She told you about me?" Cora had said she wouldn't say anything until both sides agreed to disclose their identities.

Glenys flicked away Hazel's concern. "Not you specifically. Just that we had a new witch in town. She asked if I was interested in meeting you."

Hazel's concerns didn't completely disappear with that information, though it was good to know Cora hadn't outed her. "And you said no?" If she'd said yes, Cora would have mentioned it.

"I told her I'd think about it." Glenys smiled and leaned forward in her chair. "Honestly, I was hoping to have time to figure it out on my own."

Seemed like an underhanded ploy. "Then you'd know my identity, but I wouldn't know yours."

"Exactly. With knowledge comes power. Can't be too careful in this town."

Hazel relaxed a little. She supposed that was true. Stonebridge had a proven track record, and it wasn't good where witches were concerned. "Okay, then. Now that we know about each other, what do you think?"

Glenys tapped a well-manicured finger against her lips as she studied Hazel for several moments. "I think you have formidable powers and a kind heart."

Kind heart, maybe. "Formidable powers? Why do you say that?"

She shrugged. Just my impression. "What's your lineage?"

Her lineage wasn't something she was willing to discuss at this point. She kept her features passive. "Nothing special. My mom and two aunts are witches. I learned most everything I know from them and a little from my grandmother before she passed."

Glenys quirked a brow. "Interesting that you learned spells and hexes only from them. That poses certain limitations. Any generational specialties?"

Hazel shook her head. "No hexes. We don't believe in using our powers for anything negative. I'm more interested in helping and healing, and so far, what I've learned has served me well."

The smile remained on Glenys' face, but she sensed a shift in the atmosphere. "I would say you have a lot of untapped power then. I don't mean to brag, but I'm good at detecting levels of intensity. Poor Belinda Atkins, for instance. She had the potential to become very powerful."

A shiver raced over her. "But now she's dead."

"Yes." Glenys' features turned sympathetic. "Such a waste. She never was one to do what was best for her."

"Best for her?" Hazel prodded. "Like what?"

"Like worrying more about protective spells than glamour ones. Stonebridge has some nasty entities that will do us harm if we're not careful."

Hazel's pulse thundered, and she worked to keep her expression even. "I've heard whisperings of a secret society. Mr. Winthrop that passed recently. Timothy Franklin. One other person, but his name escapes me."

Glenys snorted. "Trust me. There are others." Her gaze grew troubled, and she tapped her pen repeatedly on her desk. "That Timothy Franklin though. I worry most about him."

"Same. I picked up bad vibes from him the moment we first met."

Glenys pointed her pen at Hazel. "See? There's power behind those dark brown eyes of yours. You just need to learn to tap into it."

Hazel wasn't so sure about that, but she was thrilled at her luck in discovering Glenys and her wealth of information. She highly doubted Glenys had been this forthcoming with Peter. In fact, she'd bet her life on it. "I think Timothy tries to come across as a good guy, but he's really not, is he?"

"Don't let that friendly façade fool you. He'll kill us all if we get in his way." Uneasiness replaced Glenys' confidence that had been present in the room since Hazel had arrived. "I can't prove that it's related, but Belinda recently discovered some very interesting information about him."

This was what she'd come for. Hazel slid closer to the edge of her seat. "What was it?"

Glenys glanced out the wall of windows toward the interior of the bank. Hazel followed her gaze, but no one was close enough they could hear anything even if the door was open.

A knowing smirk lit Glenys' face. "He's a direct descendant of one of the four witches who escaped punishment that fateful night, my grandmother being another one of them. Lily Franklin."

That must be the witch Timothy had referred to when Hazel had first visited the library and he'd helped her with information about the town's history. The one he said he *wasn't* a relative.

Glenys shook her head in disgust. "All that nonsense he spouts about his connection to John Henry Parrish is a lie. He might not claim it, but he has powerful blood pumping through his veins."

Hazel swallowed. "You said your grandmother was one of the four?" One of Clarabelle's cohorts? Along with Timothy's grandmother?

A proud expression lit her face. "Oh yes, she—"

Glenys froze midsentence and widened her eyes.

"Blessed Mother. You are, too. Hardy. Clarabelle Foster Hardy. Tell me I'm wrong." She held up a hand before Hazel could answer. "No, don't bother. My intuition tells me I'm spot on, and it's never wrong."

Hazel struggled to inhale a breath. Their conversation had decimated the boundaries of her comfort zone. "Yes. Clarabelle is my ancestor."

CHAPTER FIFTEEN

Glenys sank back into her chair and regarded Hazel with a mixture of suspicion and awe. "No wonder you have such potential. If you were taught the right spells, you'd surpass me."

"No." Hazel shook her head as fear crept over her. "I'm sure that's not true." If it was, that made her position quite precarious. For one, she had a feeling Glenys liked being the most powerful witch in Stonebridge. It had obviously served her well.

Glenys laughed and then grinned. "Oh, yes. You are exactly what we need to tip the scales."

She didn't like the sound of that. "The scales?"

"Of power. Timothy proclaims he hates witches, and maybe he does, but he still uses the magic in his blood to help him weed us out and destroy us. With us working together, he wouldn't stand a chance."

The urge to run overwhelmed her. "I...I don't know. It's not the type of thing I like to get involved in. I choose to use my powers to help people."

Glenys snorted. "Who better to help than your own kind? Besides, just having you in Stonebridge enhances my powers. Can't you feel it?"

She shook her head in bewilderment. At this point, she wasn't sure of anything. "Maybe."

Glenys straightened the papers on her desk. "Don't you worry about any of that right now. The only thing I would advise is that you learn a few spells to protect yourself. If not offensive, then at least defensive."

A shiver raced over her. "I have a concealment spell to keep me from being discovered."

Glenys regarded her like one might a child. "Oh, darling. If you intend to stay here very long, you're going to need something stronger than that. I'm surprised Timothy hasn't already discovered you. I'd be happy to teach you a few of my favorites if you'd like. Or Cora could if you trust her more."

Maybe Glenys was right. She didn't have to use what she'd learned for negative purposes. Only to protect herself and her friends. "That's very kind of you to offer. Let me think about it." Though she didn't believe she'd think about it for very long. However, she did want to consult Clarabelle's spells first.

A genuine smile returned to her face. "Absolutely. You can let me know anytime. The offer stands."

A sliver of guilt nipped her for misjudging Glenys. Many witches weren't fond of sharing spells outside their families, yet she was willing. "Thank you."

Another thought landed solidly in her mind. "If Belinda had something on Timothy, then do you think it's possible he might have killed her?"

She released a heavy sigh. "He could very well be the killer. If I had to guess, that's who I'd choose."

Hazel hesitated for a wary second, and then decided to plow ahead with her questions. She and Glenys seemed to have established solid ground between them, so it seemed natural to want to be honest.

"Please don't take offense to this, Glenys, but I have to ask. I've heard rumors that your boyfriend, Grant, had been involved with

Belinda. Could that be true? I don't know Grant at all. For your sake and Belinda's, could he be capable of murder if cornered?"

Glenys burst out with a laugh, and Hazel blinked in surprise. "Oh, Blessed Mother, no. Grant has a lot of drive and ambition. You watch, that man will go places you and I could only dream of, but he has one of the kindest and loyal hearts I know. Trust me, Hazel. If he was cheating on me, I'd know."

Charlie's previous words brought an image to her mind of Grant and Belinda together at the lake. Had Charlie lied? Hazel sensed that Glenys believed he was faithful, but Grant could have conned her, too.

Not wanting to belabor the point, Hazel forced a smile. "That's good to know. I'd heard a few things and would worry if you were involved with that kind of a man."

Glenys waved away her concern, seeming genuinely confident about her remarks. "Eventually, you'll hear this anyway, so I'll tell you now. Belinda was jealous of me. She resented that the other witches in town look up to me as a leader. She hated that I received more attention and respect than she did. I tried to help her, to tell her if she'd just improve her attitude and the way she'd treated others, then the rest of us would respect her more in return.

"Instead of heeding my advice, she grew angry, blamed her troubles on me, and threatened to make me pay." Glenys snorted. "As if she could. She knew she couldn't compete with my powers, so she went after Grant. She flirted with him relentlessly in public. I think she even broke up with her boyfriend, telling him she and Grant were in love."

Hazel could attest to at least part of that. She knew Belinda was narcissistic in the worst way, so Glenys' explanation made sense. "I feel bad that her life ended as it did, but yeah, she had a way of annoying many people."

"Exactly." Glenys gave her a sad but assured nod. "She wasn't the best at hiding her witchcraft, either. If Timothy had caught wind of any of it, he'd take her out. Especially after what she'd found out about him. I worry that Cora might not be safe since she was so closely involved with her. But we're all hoping people realize her attempts to help Belinda were based strictly on an employer-employee relationship."

Hazel frowned, not liking that her friend might be in jeopardy because of her association with Belinda. She'd check in with her after she finished at the bank.

After that, Hazel had a lot to think about, including figuring out a way to help Peter discover this information without flat out telling him. If he learned on his own, that would put more credence in it plus keep Hazel's heritage in the clear.

First, she needed to finish opening her new business bank account. She glanced down at the application in front of her.

Glenys pointed to a section halfway down the page. "Don't worry about putting all your personal information on the top part. We can get that from your account. Just fill out the information regarding your business. That's all I need."

"Awesome." Hazel quickly finished the form and passed it back to Glenys.

She scanned over it. "Perfect. If it's missing anything, we'll let you know. And if there's anything else I can help with, spells or otherwise, please let me know."

Hazel stood and shook her hand, receiving a warm rush of friendliness. "Thank you. This has been great."

She'd expected to leave but, Glenys' offer of help held her back. "Actually, there is one thing. I'm interested in purchasing Clarabelle's house."

Glenys' face brightened. "Excellent idea. I know Clarabelle would love that."

"You know her?" Hazel was interested in her experiences with her grandmother.

"Oh, yes. We've had several visits. Poor lady. She carries a lot of unrest in her. Death should be a peaceful time."

Hazel nodded. "I wish I could help her."

"I'm sure having you in the house would bring her much comfort. Maybe while you're there, you can find her missing spell book."

She widened her eyes. "Her spell book? Why would you think it's still there after all this time?"

Glenys shrugged. "I feel it there. Or at least a talisman or other powerful object. But I haven't been able to locate it. There are some spells in my grandmother's book that seem incomplete. From what I can tell, she and your grandmother were the closest out of the four."

"That's very interesting." She kept her expression passive and her pulse even. "I'd love to find it, too."

"That house has been on the market for a while. I'm sure you can get a great deal. Why don't you contact a realtor, negotiate the price, and then let me know when you're ready for a loan. I can expedite it for you."

It warmed her heart to be so accepted by the witches she'd met in Stonebridge. "Thank you so much. I will do exactly that."

Hazel said her goodbyes and left Glenys' office, surprised that she'd spent more than an hour inside. She'd pop in at Cora's and then head to the teashop to give Gretta her lunch break.

As she neared the exit, the handsome and charming Mr. Brogan left his desk and met her at the front door and opened it for her. "We hope you'll come back again."

A tingle of appreciation for a chivalrous man spread through her. "I'm sure I will." She walked out with a smile on her face.

CHAPTER SIXTEEN

After being reassured by Cora that she could protect herself, Hazel left the café. She glanced toward the police station, but then turned and headed toward her teashop instead.

She would have loved nothing more than to run straight to Peter's office and tell him what she'd learned. Of course, it was mostly hearsay regarding Timothy, but she'd discovered that nuggets of truth could always be found in even the grandest stories.

Unfortunately, she couldn't tell Peter that Glenys was a witch, nor that she was one. Still, there must be a way to lead Peter to the truth.

Hazel opened the door to her shop and allowed the calming essence of it to wash over her. She'd designed it that way on purpose so that her customers would want to return again and again. She hadn't used magic, not in the way Glenys obviously had at the bank. Instead, Hazel had used gifts from the Blessed Mother to provide a soothing bath for the senses.

Smells of lavender and vanilla fragranced the air. Watercolors of outdoor gardens that she'd collected since college adorned the walls, and her favorite Zen music with accompanying Tibetan singing bowls enhanced the shopping experience. Customers were always welcome to have a cup of their favorite tea on the house, which contributed to their pleasure in the form of taste and smell.

The only sense she was missing was touch, unless they indulged in the feel of the lovely ceramic teacups and mugs. If nothing else, they were also a delight to look at.

Hazel spotted Gretta toward the far end of the shop chatting with Mrs. Lemon and Mrs. Tillens. Gretta paused her conversation and cast a quick glance at Hazel. She waved in response, letting her assistant know she could take her break at any time now.

Hazel stepped into the backroom and hung her purse and jacket on one of the pewter hooks she'd installed for that purpose. New boxes of herbs sat stacked along the back counter, and she needed to spend the afternoon crafting since their stock of Love Potion #29 had grown low. But snippets of her earlier conversation with Glenys wouldn't stop flitting through her mind.

She needed to see Peter, to talk with him.

"Hey, beautiful."

Hazel whirled at the sound of Peter's voice. "Bl...blast it all. You scared the daylights out of me." Not to mention, the fact that he'd showed up right as she was thinking of him was a little eerie.

He grinned. This wasn't the first time he'd caught her in the backroom with her head in the clouds, and she knew he loved that he could sneak up on her. "I've been missing you ever since I left your house the other night. It's hard to focus on the case."

She wouldn't tell him that she'd had fantastic dreams about him, too. But she'd enjoyed seeing them married, so happy together, and him kissing her. "I've missed you, too." Though honestly, other things had occupied a lot of her thoughts this morning.

She deserted the boxes on the back counter and moved toward him. When she reached him, she slid her arms around his waist and absorbed the delicious sensations that rocketed through her. "Funny, but I was just thinking about you."

He smiled, happiness reflecting in his green eyes. He pulled her against his solid chest, a place she dearly loved to be. "Maybe we have a psychic connection." He lifted his brows in a teasing way.

She wanted to tell him that was entirely possible but decided against it for obvious reasons. "Maybe so."

Gretta popped in to the backroom. "Heading out...oh, sorry." She laughed.

Hazel's cheeks heated. Gretta teased her every chance she got about being right about her and Peter's budding relationship. "Have a good lunch."

A teasing look flickered in her gaze. "I will, but probably not as fun as you'll have while I'm gone." She winked.

Hazel shook her head in mock disbelief. "Go before I fire you."

Her threat only drew a bigger grin from Gretta. "Yes, boss."

The second the outer door chimed indicating Gretta's departure, Peter placed his lips on hers for a heated kiss. Hazel soaked up the pleasure for as long as she dared and then pushed him away.

"Control yourself," she said with a chuckle. "I have customers out there."

He pulled her in for one more kiss. "Just wanted to tell Gretta when I see her later that she was right."

Hazel rolled her eyes but grinned. "That's because you always have to be right."

He placed a hand over his heart. "Wounded by the lady's piercing words."

"Whatever." She took a quick peek out in the shop, checking to make sure the ladies weren't ready to check out and then she turned back to Peter. "If you're so good at reading my mind, then why was I thinking about you?"

He studied her for a long moment. She was sure he meant his action to be playful, but the deep connection unnerved her. "You wanted to tell me something."

He had that right. "Tell you something?"

He nodded thoughtfully. "Something you learned."

Maybe he could read her better than she'd thought. Or maybe she was too predictable for her own good. "Okay...actually, yes I do."

She left his side and busied herself straightening the partially used containers of herbs on the shelf near him. "I heard something interesting. Not sure if it's true, but it might be worth investigating."

"Been sleuthing again?" he teased.

Guilt slammed into her, and she lifted her gaze to him. "You say that like it's a bad thing."

His expression grew serious. "It can be when I've asked you not to."

"I didn't do anything dangerous or anything to compromise the case." In fact, what she'd learned had all been very benign. She'd tell him enough to satisfy him and tempt him into looking further. "It might not even be true."

He took her hand, forcing her to keep facing him instead of fiddling with her supplies. "Are you going to tell me already?"

And...she had him. She tried not to grin. "I heard today that Belinda might have had some damning information on Timothy Franklin. That she knew something about him that he wanted to keep secret. She might have even been blackmailing him."

His gaze intensified, and she knew she'd piqued his interest. "Is that so? What exactly did she supposedly know?"

She wanted to blurt it out, but she couldn't put Timothy in danger of being persecuted as a witch. "My source didn't know. But if Belinda had been blackmailing him, that would make him a prime suspect."

A dubious expression fell over him. "You want me to investigate a man based on a rumor that has no substance?"

She held tight to a frustrated growl and shrugged instead. She wanted so much to tell him everything. Then he'd understand. "I'm only passing along what I heard. If nothing pans out on anyone else, then investigating Timothy might give you a new direction with new information."

He lifted his chin, and she could see by the look in his eye that he hadn't completely dismissed her suggestion. "Who's your source?"

She hated withholding information from him. "I can't say."

He narrowed his gaze.

"I'm sorry. I can't. It was told to me in confidence, and I don't break promises."

He placed a finger beneath her chin and tipped her face toward him. "You want me to trust what you say, but you can't trust me enough to tell me?"

She shivered under his scrutiny. "Yes."

He shook his head, but she could tell he wasn't angry. "You must think you have me wrapped around your little finger," he teased.

She bit her bottom lip and gave him a hopeful smile.

He waited several long seconds and then huffed, indicating his submission. "Fine. I'll check into it."

Happiness and victory swept through her. She stood on tiptoes and placed a flirtatious kiss on his lips. "While you're at it, make sure to check into Grant and Quentin, too."

He growled and pulled her tight against him. "I'm starting to wonder if you're in collusion with the mayor because you sound just like him."

She gave him a sheepish look. "Just trying to help."

"Just so you know, Quentin is out of it. Rock solid alibi, but we did discover he's been taking money from his grandfather, too."

She scoffed. "The nerve of him to accuse Belinda while he was doing the exact same thing."

"Agreed. The amount is awfully high, but, unfortunately, it's still within reason for providing care for Virgil."

That didn't matter to her. "I still say he's a jerk."

The bell on the front counter rang, and Hazel widened her eyes. "I'll be right there," she called to Mrs. Tillens and Mrs. Lemon.

Peter nodded toward the exit. "I'd better go, too. Can I take you to dinner this week? Maybe Friday?"

Her heart squeezed. "I'd love that."

He placed a steamy kiss on her lips before he stepped away, his departure leaving her wanting more. She fought to catch her breath as he walked into the main part of her shop.

"Afternoon, ladies," he said.

They returned his greeting. After the door chimed, they giggled, and she heard one of them whisper, "I told you he likes her."

Hazel placed her fingertips against her heated cheeks and hoped they didn't give her away.

CHAPTER SEVENTEEN

Hazel walked down the grassy row between headstones, her gaze flicking from one to another. She glanced at Cora who had her eye toward a bird hiding in the trees overhead who sang to them. "I hope you didn't think I was crazy to suggest this for our walk today."

Cora met her gaze and smiled. "Actually, I kind of like it in here. Serenity fills most of this space. We have sunshine plus a slightly cool breeze, which is perfect. And the dates on the headstones never cease to amaze me."

Hazel pointed at one nearby. "Fifteen hundred and sixty-one. That's close to five hundred years ago."

"It's hard to imagine what Stonebridge might have looked like back then. When I see old black and white photos or drawings, there's a part of me that thinks the colors during that time weren't as vivid as they are now. But they were. The wild irises would have been just as brilliant of a purple. Some roses still as red as blood."

Hazel tried to picture her town long-ago. "We'd have to knock down a lot of buildings to get it to look like it did back then."

"And erect a few log ones." Cora stopped and peered at a thin slab of rock that stood upright, if a bit tilted, in the grass.

Hazel silently read the name, birthdate and death date, all of which had been meticulously chiseled into the gray stone. Above the names, the chiseler had carved out a skull and crossbones with wings. "Seriously, though, don't you find these kinds of headstones a little ghoulish, not peaceful?"

Cora nodded. "Funny that the images they used long ago to symbolize the physical death and spirit regeneration have now been transformed to be icons of rock bands and devil-worshippers."

Hazel continued walking, and Cora followed. "People really need to learn their symbolism before they steal ideas from someone else."

"No doubt." Cora tucked a loose strand of blond hair behind her ear and glanced at Hazel. "Sort of like the pentagram on Belinda's arm."

A cloud of sadness descended upon them. "Yeah. Just like that."

"I've overheard several people in the café mention it," Cora continued. "Many are whispering about witches, which doesn't bode well for us. Nothing like a group frenzy to screw things up for everyone."

Hazel studied her. "You mean like what happened with the witches all those years ago. Do you really believe we could be in that kind of danger? Most people in town seem so nice."

Cora scoffed. "There were plenty of nice townsfolk at the end of the 1600s, too, but that didn't stop them from their heinous crimes. They believed they were justified and that it was necessary to protect themselves."

"Such a tragedy." She'd hoped times had changed and people had learned from their mistakes.

"Hey," Cora said, her face brightening. "Do you want to see a witch's grave?"

Hazel cast a quick eye around the graveyard. "Witch's grave? They allowed that here?"

"Oh, yeah." Cora tugged on her sleeve and led her to the back corner of the cemetery. A riot of wildflowers grew in the long grass surrounding the small headstone. Beautiful purples and yellows danced under the sunlight, spreading peace and beauty over the area.

But those flowers didn't grow elsewhere in the graveyard.

Hazel knelt and brushed aside the long grass that hid most of the stone. A list of names, but no dates had been chiseled. "Wait. There's more than one witch here?" She mentally read off the names, surprised to find Clarabelle's with the rest.

She lifted her gaze to Cora. "Is one of these Glenys' ancestor?"

"Glenys?" Cora seemed shocked. "Why would you ask that?"

"It's okay. I know about Glenys and her grandmother, and she knows about me. She helped me at the bank the other day and made the mistake of trying to probe me. The pinch was so sharp that I called her on it before I realized my mistake. But no worries. By the time I left, we'd become friends."

"If Glenys has such a thing," Cora muttered.

Hazel gave her a confused look. "She seemed very helpful and friendly. Offered to teach me some protective spells."

Cora seemed dubious. "Maybe so, but let me give you a word of warning. Glenys can be friendly, but she will always, *always* put herself first."

Hazel knew many people who functioned that way, and though it wasn't a trait she admired, they were good people. "I'll remember that."

"Did she invite you to coven meetings?"

"Coven meetings? No." A worm of wondering burrowed in her mind.

Cora gave her a precise nod. "Don't trust her, Hazel. Plenty of those in the coven are searching for ways to even out the power in the group so she doesn't have it all."

Hazel shrugged, not wanting to doubt her new friend. "Maybe she wanted to get everyone else's approval before inviting me, like you did."

She snorted. "Hardly. It's not in Glenys' nature to consider others. If she thinks you belong, she'll introduce you. She believes she knows what's best for us all."

Hazel had to ask. "If that's true, then do you think she might be capable of murder? Maybe she thought that was what was best for all of us?"

Cora pondered that thought for a long moment and then sighed. "No, I don't think so. As bossy as she is, she believes we're all stronger together. Plus, the town drowned her ancestor. I don't think she'd mock her death by killing Belinda the same way. She can be highfalutin, but she's not a murderer."

"Hmm...maybe not." Hazel wasn't sure what to believe anymore. The energy she'd experienced with Glenys had been friendly and strong. But she did trust Cora more. "I'll be careful, then."

Her friend pointed a finger at her. "You be sure you do that. And if you want someone to teach you a good protective spell, let me, okay?"

"Okay." She still wanted to check Clarabelle's book, but she might as well start with Cora since she was actually breathing and could offer better feedback and corrections if necessary. After her previous, mostly unsuccessful attempts at new spells, she wouldn't mind some hands-on instruction.

Hazel returned her gaze to the headstone. "Why is Clarabelle on here? I thought no one knew what happened to her. Are her friends here, too?"

"The village did it to calm the townsfolk, I believe. They probably wanted everyone to forget that those witches had disappeared and make them think Satan had claimed them that day."

"The people here must have been naïve and or crazy."

Cora chuckled. "Many of them still are."

Hazel stood and brushed grass from her hands and knees. She considered mentioning what she'd learned about Belinda blackmailing Timothy, but now didn't seem to be the time.

Instead, she turned the topic to something happier. "A weird thing happened to me today. Actually, a couple of times recently. I was thinking about Peter, and he magically showed up. I love coincidences like that, don't you, and feeling like we're sort of synchronized somehow?"

Disbelief spread over Cora's face. "You're kidding, right?"

She shrugged, confused. "No. Why would I?"

"Oh, Hazel. I feel like your mother did you a great disservice by withholding things from you. Or perhaps it was her mother before her."

She didn't like the uncertainty that Cora's words inspired. "What do you mean?"

"That was no coincidence, silly. Witches, especially earth witches form bonds very quickly with those they like. Threads in your tapestry with him are already strengthening."

Panic tightened her chest. "Threads in our tapestry? What kind of nonsense is that?"

"It's a thing. I promise. Do an online search. All kinds of information on it."

Not good. "Why didn't you tell me this before? How do I stop it?"

Cora took her hand and infused her with a calming feeling. "It's okay, Hazel. Relax. It's a normal thing that happens when you fall in love. That's why breaking up hurts so much."

This was not happening. "I'm not falling in love."

"Okay." Her friend might have agreed in words, but her eyes suggested otherwise.

"I'm not. I swear."

Cora gave her a knowing smile but didn't continue to argue.

"Are we done here? I think we're done here." The need to escape was strong. She turned and strode toward the gate that led into the outside world, frustrated with her feelings. This was ridiculous.

After they'd left the cemetery, Hazel cast an angry glance at her friend. "Why didn't you say something sooner?"

Cora turned her palms toward Hazel. "I'd intended to if things grew serious, but you kept denying you liked him."

"And then when I came clean?" she challenged.

"I still should have had time. Usually it's months before things like this happen."

Her heart threatened to explode from fear. "*Things like this?*"

Cora expelled a breath. "Most relationships take a long time for true, strong threads to develop. Yours didn't." She paused for a long moment. "Most times when things progress like this, it suggests you may have known each other in another life. That, or the stars are adamant that you be together."

"Cora, we *can't* be together." The words exploded from her mouth, and she was grateful they were in a deserted part of town. "You know this. I'm a witch," she said through gritted teeth. "And he hates witches."

She placed a hand on Hazel's arm, slowing their pace. "Yes, I know these things. But I also know the universe doesn't make mistakes. You're going to have to trust in that."

Hazel started walking again and tried to regain control over her world. Her...and Peter? Not just fun and flirtatious? How could that ever be?

CHAPTER EIGHTEEN

Hazel had just taken her first sip of Magic Morning tea when her phone rang. If that was her mother, she'd hear about it. For as long as she could remember, she'd insisted that mornings were her meditation time, and she didn't want to be disturbed. Didn't matter. Her mother always assumed what she had to say was more important.

She lifted her phone, not recognizing the unfamiliar but local number showing on her screen. She answered it with a wary hello.

"Hazel? It's Glenys." Her voice sounded breathless, almost desperate. "I need your help."

The tone in Glenys' voice ignited her panic. "What's wrong?"

"I can't tell you over the phone. Can you meet me at Clarabelle's house? Like now?"

She glanced at the clock on the microwave. "Of course. I can be there in ten."

"Please hurry, Hazel. I think you're the only one who can help me."

Hazel ended the call and hurried to get dressed. As she drove along the tree-lined streets toward Hemlock, her mind tumbled with possible scenarios, but she couldn't come up with anything plausible.

She hesitated to park by Clarabelle's house for fear of what people would think, but if she ended up buying the place, then they'd know anyway. Still, she kept her car closer to the sacred grove than the house.

Glenys' was nowhere in sight. No car, no person.

As she walked toward Clarabelle's house, she opened her senses, searching for anything that might alert her to danger. She didn't believe Glenys would harm her, but Cora had warned her to be careful.

Nothing came across for several moments, and then she picked up on a tiny thread of fear. As she reached the front porch, the emotion grew stronger, but still no sign of Glenys.

She tested the doorknob, but it remained locked. Hazel knew she could open it by a simple request, but she wasn't so sure that Glenys could. Instead of choosing that option, she stepped off the porch and headed around back.

She found Glenys sitting on the back step with her arms wrapped tightly around her. She startled when Hazel approached, and a wave of fear nearly bowled her over. Dark shadows hovered beneath red-rimmed eyes, and her hair looked like she'd just climbed out of bed.

Hazel strode forward. "Glenys. What's wrong? How can I help?"

Glenys stood and held out her hand. Hazel took it, accepting some of the fear present there. Glenys opened her mouth, but her words dissolved into anguished sobs. She tried several times before she succeeded. "G...G...Grant is dead."

Hazel inhaled a shocked breath. *"What? How?"*

Glenys shook her head repeatedly. "I don't know. He was at my house last night until late, maybe two or three in the morning. Then he said he needed to get home because he had a phone interview with a law firm in New York. I wished him good luck and kissed him goodbye." Her voice faltered.

Hazel squeezed her hand and gave her a moment to collect herself.

Tremors vibrated from Glenys' fingers. "They found him dead in his car still outside my house. I was only yards away when someone took his life, when he breathed his last breath." She sank back to the porch step as if her legs would no longer support her.

The news left Hazel unsteady, too, so she sat next to her. She searched for words to console Glenys, but nothing that seemed appropriate surfaced.

"I'm afraid I'm next," Glenys whispered.

Fear struck hard. *"No."* She couldn't believe that.

Glenys nodded emphatically. "The police woke me this morning to question me. Someone found him in his car and called them. I was outside when they removed his body. Oh, Blessed Mother." She choked on a sob.

Hazel wrapped an arm around her shoulders. "Breathe, Glenys. Just breathe."

Her body shuddered as she took several breaths before she calmed again. "I saw him Hazel. As they dragged him from his car. There was...there was an inverted pentagram on his cheek. Black as the night."

Hazel covered her mouth with her hand as a similar image on Belinda's body came to mind. She could see exactly where this would go. "They'll say a witch did it."

Trepidation radiated in her eyes. "Worse. I think I might be next."

"Why would you think that?"

"Think about it. Belinda died because she was blackmailing Timothy."

That explained one death. "Okay, but why would he or the group of them kill Grant?"

"Because Grant knew, too. Belinda told him. That's how I learned."

That meant there was some sort of relationship between Grant and Belinda, whether Glenys was willing to admit it or not.

She gripped Hazel's hand. "They're going to kill me, too."

"They might not know that he told you."

Glenys shook her head in disbelief. "He might have said something before they killed him. Even if he didn't, it's not a far stretch to think that he'd tell his girlfriend. I'm in danger. I can feel it."

Hazel couldn't let her fall apart now. "It's okay. You have protection spells."

"What if I don't see them coming? My powers are strong, but I'm not completely invincible."

Then Glenys had one option. "You have to go to the police."

She looked at Hazel like she'd lost her mind. *"I can't tell them I'm a witch."*

"No. Listen. You don't have to. You only have to say that Grant told you information about Timothy."

She shook her head vehemently. "I can't. Some in town already suspect me. I can't be anywhere near this. I need you to go to the police for me."

"Me? Why would they listen to me?"

"You're involved with Peter. He'll listen."

"This has gone far beyond Peter. The feds are involved. I expect they'll be more so since Grant was the mayor's nephew."

Glenys blanched. She lifted the purse sitting near her feet and opened it, removing a white envelope. "Take this. Tell Peter an anonymous person gave it to you."

Hazel hesitated to take the envelope and shook her head. "You tell them."

Glenys shoved it at her. "Tell them you'd suspected Belinda was a witch. Tell them she'd been blackmailing Timothy. Then give them this. It's a document I managed to procure several years ago. A roster of the Sons of Stonebridge."

"Sons of Stonebridge?"

"The ones who want us all dead. It will prove that Timothy has taken an oath to kill witches. That makes it doubly damning for him. He needs to be behind bars. That's the only way I'll be safe." She inhaled a quick breath. "The only way any of us will be safe."

Before Hazel could argue again, Glenys stood. "I'll be staying with Harriett for a few days. Until it's safe to be by myself again. Please take that to Peter and help us all." She sniffed as she turned and strode away, her body tight and her footsteps swift.

Hazel stared at the letter in her hand and then turned over the envelope to find it hadn't been sealed. She slid out the document. The worn piece of paper looked as though it had been opened and refolded many times.

She scanned the words. The original charter of the Sons of Stonebridge, created seven years ago, stated that each member pledged to erase witches from this world. They would give their life to do so and protect the salvation of mankind at any cost.

She swallowed past the hard lump in her throat.

At the end of the paragraph, four names had been typed, paired with the signatures of each men. Timothy Franklin, Samuel Canterbury, Albert Winthrop, and, Blessed Mother help her...John Bartles.

She didn't know for sure that the John Bartles listed was the same as one of Peter's officers. John was a popular name after all. But if it wasn't him, it could likely be one of his relatives.

Hazel closed her eyes for a long moment, cursing the crazy, messed up world she lived in. The men listed on that page had sworn to give their lives to ensure that she and her kind would die, and her heart struggled to accept that.

She liked John. He'd been nothing but kind and decent toward her.

Anxiety churned in her stomach as she folded the paper and placed it back in the envelope. She'd have to show it to Peter. There was no other way. If she refused and those men did kill Glenys, she'd never forgive herself.

Coming forward with this information might place her in a precarious position with Peter. She would have to be extra careful with her words and expressions. She couldn't slip up.

She'd have to blame everything on her source. He'd accept that.

She stood and considered popping in to visit Clarabelle while she was at the house but decided against it. She needed to take care of this nasty business as soon as possible and wouldn't sleep until she did.

Probably not after, either.

CHAPTER NINETEEN

Hazel parked her Honda in front of the police station and stepped out. She tried not to think about the state of her hair as she entered the building. A so-called messy bun and yoga pants looked sexy on some women. Not her. But Glenys' frantic phone call hadn't given her time to worry about anything else.

Margaret sat at her desk outside Peter's office, rocking a hippie look including braided hair with a suede headband across her forehead, a red patterned, loose-flowing blouse, and so many beads. "Morning, girlfriend. It's nice to see a friendly face for once."

She chuckled, even though her insides churned. "Peter said it's been kind of crazy around here lately with the feds."

"Crazy is an understatement."

Hazel gestured toward Peter's office. "Is he available for a few minutes?"

A wry smile crossed Margaret's lips. "I'd say he's always available where you're concerned. Go on back."

She rolled her eyes but smiled. "Thanks."

Her guts churned, and if she didn't know better, she'd swear she had a fever. Anxiety had a way of throwing her entire body off balance.

But this had to be done. No looking back.

She knocked softly on Peter's open door and stepped inside.

His immediate and bright grin only added to her apprehension. "Hey. I was just thinking about you."

Oh, great. More threads weaving together in their tapestry.

He stood and met her at the side of his desk where he placed a sweet kiss on her lips. She wished she was in a place to appreciate it.

"I need to talk to you." Her heart hammered. "Is your office okay, or are there...others who might hear?"

"Meaning the feds?"

She nodded.

"They won't be in until ten. I'll shut my door anyway."

Hazel remembered exactly how well raised voices penetrated that door and made a note to be sure she kept her voice low.

When they were both seated on opposite sides of the desk, she pulled the envelope from her purse and presented it to Peter.

He frowned. "What's this?"

"You know how we've talked in the past about a secret anti-witch society," she said in lowered tones. "And I said that Timothy might have killed Belinda because she was blackmailing him?"

"Yes." He unfolded the paper and scanned it, his eyebrows digging trenches in his forehead.

She pointed toward it. "That is an official document from the group I told you about. You can see they are original signatures. One of your officers is listed there, too. John Bartles."

He nodded slowly and then met her gaze. "I'm still not following you here."

She worried that he didn't seem upset in the least that the society existed or that a member was on his police force. "I've heard rumors that Belinda was a witch. I'm sure you could check her house if you wanted and find some sort of proof to that fact." Blessed Mother forbid anyone ever check her house.

Surprise flashed in his eyes. "Now you're calling her a witch? The lady who's always against that sort of thing?"

She wanted to defend herself, but she only nodded.

He returned his gaze to the document and repeatedly nodded. She waited several long minutes while the man processed her information.

"Well?" she finally asked.

His green eyes flashed with interest when he met her gaze. "I'm not sure how to present this information to the others. This document obviously shows Timothy's intent toward witches, or at least what he thought of them seven years ago. But proving that he knew Belinda was a witch will be difficult without his admission or a witness who can and will testify to that fact."

Disappointment steamrolled her. "That's it?"

He lifted both hands. "Don't get upset, Hazel. This is great information that we could maybe use. But it gets into those gray areas this town has always struggled with."

Gray areas? Was he referring to the lives of people who lived outside his box?

Her throat tightened, making it hard to breathe.

"Even if we can't use this, I think you'll be happy to know that my men are picking up Timothy as we speak."

Wait. What? "Did you find other evidence against him?"

He tapped his fingertips on his desk in a restless manner. "We found several electronic transfers to Belinda's account for the same amount that coincided on the same day as the withdrawals from Timothy's. The feds obtained a warrant and had the bank pull records that show in fact those transfers went into Belinda's account."

Relief washed over her. Glenys and the rest of the witches in town, including her would be safe tonight. Her throat eased, and she inhaled a deep breath. "That's...really good news."

Peter leaned back in his chair and examined her. "We have you and your 'source' to thank for that lead."

Her source. The thought of how many people had been combined to become her source was insane. Again, guilt pricked her for not telling the whole truth. Was that another of those gray areas?

Still, this was good news. "I'm so relieved to hear you've caught him." She hadn't realized how much this case had bothered her. It had hit a little too close to home, closer than she'd been willing to admit. She'd wanted to believe the other witches in town were the ones in danger, and that she was still sort of an outsider, protected by anonymity. But that really wasn't the case anymore.

A sly smile curved his kissable lips. "Want to tell me who your source is now?"

Her reprieve fled. "No. You know I can't. I promised."

He leaned forward, capturing her with his gaze. "I have to be honest, Hazel. I don't like secrets between us."

The need to defend herself kicked in even though he hadn't directly accused her of anything. "I don't like them, either, but you also haven't told me everything you know."

The worst thing was the Blessed Mother knew she wanted to tell him every detail about her and have him accept her as she was.

"Yes, but mine is official police business."

She had legitimate reasons, too. "And mine is an ethical and moral choice."

He gave a low growl of frustration. "Fine. I understand. But I feel like you should trust me more."

That hurt. "I do trust you."

"Some," he argued. "But I get this overwhelming sense that you're holding back. And I don't mean just about the case."

Unexpected and unwanted sadness bubbled inside her, making it hard to breathe again. It was like she'd found the perfect guy, but he couldn't be the perfect guy for her.

She met his gaze and held it. "I'm sorry, Peter. I don't mean to shut you out. It's just hard to open up to people sometimes." She didn't know if she ever truly could with him.

He reached across the desk and took her hand. Familiar electrical energy coursed through her. Where it normally excited her, this time it brought comfort. "I will never do anything to hurt you, okay?"

She blinked rapidly and nodded. How she wished she could believe him.

A knock at the door brought their tender moment to a halt.

Peter stood and opened his office door. Sargent Gentry peeked in, nodded at Hazel and then faced his boss. "Franklin's coming in right now. Do you want him here in your office or in an interrogation room?"

"Put him in the interrogation room." Peter glanced to her. "I'll walk you out, Hazel."

He didn't take her hand as they left, and she was grateful. Sometimes, he could be flirtatious at his office. But now, he was all business.

Hazel hadn't made it to the door when two officers entered, each holding on to one of Timothy's handcuffed arms. The librarian's usual white button-down shirt had come completely untucked, and his glasses seemed askew on his face. His cheeks were crimson, and anger burned in his gaze, but an underlying sense of fear came through, too.

He caught sight of Peter and hurled an accusing glare at him. "This is a mistake, Parrish. I didn't do anything to Belinda Atkins."

Peter's expression remained calm, and he nodded to Hazel. "I'll see you later," he said in a lowered voice.

He turned toward Timothy and jerked his head toward a room down the hall. "Let's talk, Timothy. I believe you have some information that could help us." Peter walked away without a backward glance.

Something in Timothy's demeanor bothered her, but she couldn't pinpoint what. All she knew was she needed fresh air and to give nature a chance to soothe her soul. She would leave her car parked where it was and walk to her teashop.

Outside, a crowd of people had gathered around the entrance to the police station. A buzz from their conversations greeted her, and suddenly, all eyes were on her.

Lachlan Brogan from the bank trapped her gaze. "Are they arresting him for Belinda's murder?"

Several voices piped in to ask the same question, and their frenzied interest slammed Hazel like a punch. "I don't know." She glanced at the many faces. "I only heard Chief Parrish say he wanted to talk to Timothy."

"Nothing else?" Mrs. Lemon asked.

"You must have heard something," another man said.

She shook her head and pushed her way through the crowd. "I'm sorry. I don't know."

At the back of the group, Hazel found Cora watching her with trepidation. Cora slipped her arm through Hazel's and directed her away from the crowd. They didn't stop when they reached Cora's Café, but continued until they stood on a rock bridge several blocks from the center of town.

Blessed water, fresh with spring runoff, rushed beneath their feet. Hazel inhaled pure energy, and Cora released her arm.

"I think Peter's making a mistake," Cora said in a hushed tone even though they were completely alone.

Hazel drew her brows together. "By arresting Timothy? You know as well as I do that he hates witches. In fact, it seems common knowledge."

She shrugged, looking like she might cry. "I'm pretty sure he didn't do it."

Hazel didn't understand. "How can you know this?"

She visibly swallowed and dropped her gaze from Hazel to the river below. "Because I was at his house the night the murder happened."

Her brain faltered. "You were...with Timothy? *Why?*" She couldn't begin to fathom how her friend could be involved with such a man.

Cora flicked her gaze back to Hazel, her face flushed. "I wasn't *with* him. Please. You'll make me sick. I was in his house. While he was asleep."

Everything she said spun Hazel's head faster. "Wait. Slow down. You were in his house while he was asleep? *Are you crazy?* Why would you do such a thing?"

She folded her arms tight against her. "I'll admit it wasn't the smartest thing I've ever done, but the coven has been desperate to check his house for his ancestor's book of spells."

This made no sense. "Don't you think his family would have burned it all those years ago when they denounced his grandmother and let the village take her?"

"Maybe. Probably. But Glenys has been pushing boundaries lately, and since she's the only one with an original book of spells, she's the only one who can access the most powerful ones."

Except Hazel knew that Glenys wasn't the only one with a spell book.

Cora tucked a loose strand of hair behind her ear. "Most in the coven feel we need a way to balance out her power. So, I gave Timothy a concoction when he was in the café for dinner. Something that was slow-acting, so that he'd have enough time to get home, and then after the café closed I went and searched."

"You're crazy. Why didn't you tell me? I thought we were friends." That part hurt the most. It seemed no one in this town felt safe enough to trust another.

Cora gave her a pained look. "I do trust you. Of course, I do. But this was coven business, and I didn't feel like I could talk about it with you."

At first, Hazel had thought she might want to be part of this group, but now she wasn't so sure.

Hazel exhaled, searching for calm in all this craziness. "Okay, let's slow this down and take it piece by piece. What time did Timothy leave the café?"

She placed two fingers near her temple and closed her eyes. "He left about thirty minutes before I closed at nine."

"And you arrived at his house at...?"

"I was there by nine-thirty. Possibly earlier because I was in a hurry to close."

Hazel fought to keep anger out of her words. "You're right. He couldn't have done it. The coroner guessed the time of death to be around one in the morning. If you were there by nine-thirty and were there most of the night, there's no way he could have done it."

Cora closed her eyes, and her chin trembled.

Hazel wanted to show mercy, but it wouldn't come. "I can't believe this. Peter has just arrested an innocent man. Well, at least one innocent of this crime. On one hand, it would be nice to let him rot in jail so we don't have to worry about his threatening presence. But if that happens, the killer will remain free. One who might be more dangerous to us than Timothy. What a mess."

Hazel swiveled, leaned against the side of the bridge and turned her face toward the warmth of the sun. "You obviously can't tell Peter you were in Timothy's house."

"No," Cora said in a defeated tone.

"So that leaves us up a creek." *Son of a biscuit.* She'd thought she had this figured out. Now they were all in danger once again.

Cora tipped her head against Hazel's shoulder. "I'm so sorry."

They both remained lost in their thoughts for several minutes. Hazel tried many paths to find a way to resolve their dilemma, but none would work.

Except...

She heaved a sigh. "The only way out of this is to find the true killer."

Cora lifted her head and looked at Hazel. "How will we ever do that? The feds haven't been able to crack the case for Belinda, let alone whoever committed Grant's murder."

Hazel thought of telling her about Glenys' frantic call and resulting meeting, but Cora had damaged her trust for the time being. "We start at the beginning and go through every detail again. I'll start with Charlie."

Cora blew out a breath. "Are you sure? If he is the killer, he might become dangerous."

"Don't worry. I'm not going to do anything stupid. I'll invite him to meet me at the café where there are plenty of people and the police station is only a holler away."

CHAPTER TWENTY

Getting Charlie to agree to meet her at Cora's for afternoon pie had been a breeze for Hazel. All she had to do was mention she had information on Belinda's murder, and he agreed to meet her. She still hated to think sweet Charlie could do such a thing, but love did crazy things to people.

She arrived fifteen minutes before Charlie was scheduled to show and spotted Cora sitting at a table with Lachlan Brogan. They both seemed to be in good spirits. Hazel headed toward them. When she encountered higher than normal energy swirling between them, she paused.

Cora laughed, and Hazel realized they were flirting with each other.

The second she considered turning away so she wouldn't interrupt them, Lachlan looked up and caught her gaze. He glanced at Cora and spoke, and then Cora turned her way.

Hazel gave a small wave, and Cora motioned her forward. She pasted on a smile and hoped she hadn't interrupted any new developments in Cora's previously non-existent love life. "Hey, guys."

Cora's cheeks were flushed, and she seemed happier than she had in a long time. "Hi, Hazel. I didn't expect to see you so soon."

Hazel gave Lachlan a cursory smile before she glanced back at her friend. "Last minute thing. I'm meeting a friend for pie."

"Funny," Lachlan said. "I'm doing the same. Meeting my uncle."

Cora gave a nonchalant chuckle. "I was just keeping Lachlan company until he arrived."

He gestured with his chin toward the café's entrance. "There he is right now."

Hazel swiveled her head and then smiled. "I didn't know Luca was your uncle." She remembered he'd mentioned he had family in town, but she'd thought he'd made that up so he'd have a reasonable excuse to be in Stonebridge after Dotty Fingleton's pearls went missing.

Lachlan seemed surprised. "You know my uncle?"

Before she could answer, Luca approached the table and gave her a wide smile. "Bella Hazel. How good to see you."

She allowed him to kiss her on both cheeks. "Good to see you, too. I thought you and Dotty were on a whirlwind tour of Europe."

His expression dimmed. "Sadly, we had to return home too soon. The nuns kicked her daughter out of school. We could have left her to survive on her own, but her mother has a soft heart. Softer than she wants anyone to know."

He turned his gaze to Cora. "I see my nephew understands the value of a woman who can cook." He laughed.

Cora's cheeks grew redder, and she stood. "Oh, no. We were just chatting while he waited for you." She stepped aside and gestured for Luca to sit.

Luca shook his head. "You ladies must join us."

"I can't," Cora said quickly. "Work calls."

"Me, either," Hazel added. "I'm actually meeting a friend, too. But I'd love to catch up another time." Though Peter wouldn't be happy to know that.

"Our loss," Lachlan said, exuding some of his uncle's charm. But without the foreign accent, it didn't hold quite the same power.

Hazel wished them both well, and then snagged Cora's hand and pulled her toward the kitchen.

"Is it Charlie that you're meeting?" Cora asked.

Hazel nodded. "No time like the present. I've decided the best approach is to confront him directly. Please keep an eye on us, and call for help if anything seems amiss."

Cora nodded, her features grim. She slid a hand beneath her collar and pulled a long chain from beneath her shirt. A dull silver medallion swung from the end of it. "Put this on. It's very old and carries powerful protection."

Before Hazel could question more or decline, Cora slid it over her head. "You'll want to conceal it. Others might try to take it from you if they know you have it."

A shiver of knowing passed over her. Something instinctual inside her agreed that, indeed, the talisman carried great strength. She lifted the medallion and tucked it inside her shirt. "I really hope I won't need it."

"Me, too."

"If you could keep other customers away from us, that would be great."

Hazel gave her a quick hug before she re-entered the dining area. Just as she emerged, Charlie walked through the front door. She caught his attention and headed toward him.

"Hey, Hazel." He didn't carry a smile with him today. She couldn't blame him. "Want to sit here?"

She shook her head. "The back will be better. More private. We don't need our conversation being the talk of the town." Nor did she want everyone telling Peter who she'd been seen with.

Cora seemed sufficiently composed and friendly when she took their orders and then brought their slices of pie. "Enjoy."

Hazel wished she could pull her back and ask her to sit with them for support, but if Charlie freaked out, she'd need someone to get help.

Hazel lifted her fork, but Charlie left his on the table.

"You said you had information about Belinda."

She sighed and met his gaze. It seemed neither one would be enjoying the temptations on the table before her, and that was a big shame. "I don't know how to say this other than come right out with what I know."

He tipped his head in agreement. "I like a straight shooter."

She shivered at the word, shooter. "I recently had a conversation with Glenys."

He snorted in disgust and shook his head. "She's up to no good."

Hazel shrugged. "She said the same about you."

A frown creased his forehead. "What do you mean?"

She wasn't sure she could flat out lie to the man, but she needed to say something. Blessed Mother help and protect her. "Glenys says you killed Belinda. That she has proof."

His fists landed on the table with a thud loud enough to stop her heart. "I'll kill her."

She glanced to Cora who watched with a wide-eyed, questioning gaze. She shook her head slightly and then refocused on Charlie. "It's okay. It's okay. I don't believe her. I wanted to give you a heads-up before she goes to the police." Maybe that threat would keep him from doing any harm to her.

He scrubbed a cupped palm over his mouth and shook his head. "She's a vile, vindictive creature. She can't get away with this."

She worked to send calming vibes his way. They did little to lessen the intense vibrations rocketing off him, and she worried she may have gone too far with her meddling this time. "I'm sorry. I didn't mean to upset you like this."

"You don't understand," he said in a harsh whisper. "Glenys is the most powerful witch in Stonebridge. She wasn't about to be usurped by a woman like Belinda who abused glamour and went against the coven. She's the one who killed her."

Hazel placed a hand over her mouth to cover her shock. "Are you saying you know this for a fact?"

He gave her a swift and bitter nod.

She leaned closer to whisper. "Then why didn't you tell the police?"

He looked at her like she was an imbecile. "Because I didn't want to end up dead, too. She doesn't know what I know. If she did, I'd be dead already. Grant knew too much and look what happened to him."

She shook her head. "I don't understand. Glenys said she and Grant loved each other, and she didn't believe he'd be unfaithful. But, there's the rumors about him and Belinda. I don't know what is true and what's not."

He shifted a glance from side to side, checking their surroundings. "I think Grant may have loved Glenys, but he messed up. Belinda had power and knew how to use glamour to manipulate others with it including Grant. If she'd had enough time, she could have been unstoppable in all areas."

Hazel placed fingers on both her temples to try to stop the throbbing. "Are you saying you think Glenys killed Belinda because she was threatened by what she might become?" If that was true, Hazel herself could be in danger from Glenys.

"That was part of it. But also, Belinda knew what Glenys had planned, and she disagreed with her. Said she couldn't let her go through with it."

She lifted her palms to him. "Okay. Slow down. You're losing me here."

"Belinda liked all kinds of people, whether they were magical or not." A bolt of genuine pain flashed in his eyes. "I'd like to think she really did love me and that she broke up with me to keep me out of this mess."

"She didn't love Grant?"

He shrugged. "I think she loved the idea of stealing Grant and sticking it to Glenys. But mostly, I think she loved herself, and she wanted Glenys' power."

Hazel could believe that part.

He swallowed, causing his Adam's apple to bob in his throat. "I don't know why I'm telling you this. Please, please don't say anything."

"Of course, Charlie. I'd never say anything to put you in danger. If anyone asks, this was strictly a landscaping design meeting. I promise."

He exhaled and focused a sharp gaze on her. "Glenys wants to take over the town, Hazel. Kill anyone who might be the slightest threat to her."

She could see in his expression that he meant what he said, but... "She couldn't do that." Though Hazel wouldn't be surprised to learn that she'd threatened to do so.

"Belinda thought she was capable, said she was only missing one piece of a spell. Something that the original witches created."

Hazel shook her head repeatedly, and her veins iced over. "No. I can't believe that much power is possible." Though in her heart, she feared it was.

He shrugged. "I don't know much about that world. I only know Belinda feared that might happen, and now she's dead."

She lifted the glass of water Cora had brought with their pie and downed the contents. The drink did little to calm her fears, but it did help with her constricted throat. "Now what?"

His fear and hopelessness reached out to her. "Don't know. I've thought about leaving town, but my whole life is here. And what if Belinda was worried for nothing?"

Hazel wasn't sure it was for nothing since she was dead, but saying that wouldn't help Charlie.

"Sorry I told you all that. Part of me hoped you could help since you're dating the chief. But it's not like he could help anyway."

"If he could prove Glenys killed her, he could send her to prison."

"I have a hard time believing that will happen."

Hazel wasn't so sure, either.

Charlie scooted to the edge of the booth. "I'm going to go, Hazel. Forget I told you any of this. Keep your head down and run whenever you hear the word 'witch'. Life is safer that way."

He didn't stick around for her to attempt to console him. He nodded at Cora as he paid and then he strolled from the café. By his casual stride, most would think he was happy-go-lucky, but she knew very well what churned inside him.

She sat for several long moments, staring at her pie, trying to center her thoughts.

Holy harpies. If what he said was true...

She couldn't go there. Couldn't allow herself to picture that scenario.

Cora slid into the other side of the booth, her jeans whooshing across the vinyl seat. "I'm so glad I didn't have to call Peter. I was worried there for a while."

She shook her head, her thoughts scrambling through information. "No, he was fine."

She snorted. "He didn't seem fine."

Hazel inhaled and focused on her friend. As much as she believed she trusted Cora, she couldn't mention what Charlie had told her, not if there was the smallest chance it might cost him his life.

She relaxed her features. "Well, he wasn't happy with me asking lots of questions about Belinda, but in the end, I still believe he loved her and wouldn't hurt her."

Cora nodded, seeming satisfied. "On to Quentin, then?"

It would be best if Cora thought so. "I think that's a great next step. Maybe I'll have a casual chat with his grandpa when he comes for breakfast in the morning. He might be able to tell us all kinds of things about his grandson that Quentin wouldn't want us to know."

"Great. If you interview him here, I can help, too."

Hazel purposely glanced at her watch. "I need to get to work. I'll call you later."

Cora walked with her to the door and hugged her goodbye. Hazel slipped out into the beautiful sunshine, wondering how such dark and devious things could happen in a town that seemed so serene.

CHAPTER TWENTY-ONE

The hollowness of being alone in her sleuthing endeavors weighed heavily on Hazel as she sat at her kitchen table the following morning. She arranged with Gretta to handle the morning customers and then called Cora to say interviewing Virgil Fletcher would have to wait one more day.

She couldn't talk to Cora about what she knew. For one, it might put her in danger with Glenys, or two, while she didn't think Cora confided in Glenys, at this point, Hazel wasn't sure what to believe about any of them.

Worse, she couldn't talk to Peter because he couldn't know or wouldn't understand everything at play.

One day, she'd learn to mind her own business. If she hadn't started poking around, she wouldn't have any of this information about Belinda's death. She could have been happy and much safer in her oblivion.

At least, she hoped she would have.

Still, if Glenys was as powerful as everyone believed, she might have discovered Hazel and her heritage anyway, long before Hazel learned anything about the threat of her. Charlie had mentioned Glenys was searching for a missing component for her dark spell. Hazel feared she might find it in Clarabelle's book.

One person couldn't accomplish the horrible feat without the other. It must have been a safety thing back when they'd created it.

Maybe, if another witch besides them discovered one of the spell books, the separation of components would make it so she couldn't complete the spell on her own.

Hazel wished she knew.

She could make a trip to the house to ask Clarabelle, but she had a feeling that would be opening a bigger can of worms, and she had all she could handle at the moment.

She still wasn't one hundred percent sure Glenys was guilty. For all she knew, Belinda had fed lies to Cora and Charlie, turning them against Glenys.

Hazel lifted her teacup to her lips and the scent of Majestic Mint tickled her senses, bringing her back to the moment. The first thing she needed to do was see if she could prove Glenys had told her the truth or lied. If she could find the book of spells belonging to Glenys' ancestor, she'd be off to a good start.

If Cora was right and Glenys did have it and therefore, access to the spells it contained, Hazel could continue down that vein of investigation.

A thump coming from her left stole her attention, and she found Mr. Kitty sitting on the chair next to her, Clarabelle's tome beneath his front paws.

"I don't have time for studying this morning."

You'll need this.

She frowned. "What?"

Take the book with you to Glenys' house. It will help.

She stared at her cat for a long moment, dumbfounded. She had no idea how taking the book to Glenys' would help her discover the killer or if Glenys also had an ancient book of spells. She flicked several glances between the book and Mr. Kitty. "I don't understand."

You will. Go now.

"Now?" She couldn't decide on the fly like this to break and enter. She needed time to create a plan and mentally prepare herself.

She glanced at the clock. Nine-thirty. Glenys should be at the bank right now. It was unlikely Glenys would carry the tome around with her. "What if she's left the book at her friend Harriett's?" she asked her cat.

Go. Now.

A sharp pain throbbed between her temples, but Hazel stood anyway. She must be certifiable to attempt to break into someone's home, more so to trust a cat that communicated telepathically, who also hated her. But she was going to do it.

* * *

Hazel went by bike even though storm clouds were building on the horizon. She'd picked a slower mode of transportation, for sure, but people were used to seeing her riding around town. Plus, a bike would be easier to hide while she was in the house, as opposed to her very noticeable car parked anywhere near Glenys' home. If it rained on her while she was out, she'd survive.

The bike ride to the cottage on Primrose seemed to take forever, and yet was over in an instant. She'd already checked at the bank to make sure Glenys' BMW sedan was there before she headed this way, but that did little to settle her anxiety.

She wheeled past the eighteenth-century house with its black pitched roof and wild roses climbing up the exterior. Plenty of oaks and pines provided a barrier between the street and her cottage, but there was enough visibility that she'd still feel vulnerable.

Several hundred yards down the deserted street, when she'd spotted no one outside, she turned back and pedaled toward Glenys' home. She wanted to be out of sight as soon as possible.

Once she reached the driveway, she didn't hesitate to turn in. Her tires whooshed along the cement drive as she pedaled fast. She continued toward the house as if she'd been invited, and after a quick glance behind her, she stowed her bike behind a tree where it would be less likely to be seen.

Her breaths came fast from that last sprint.

She placed a hand over her midsection like an expectant mother protecting her baby to ensure the tome she'd tucked beneath her shirt was still safe and secure.

She still had no idea why she'd needed to bring it, but if Mr. Kitty had been around for hundreds of years, maybe he knew a thing or two.

She stopped short at the front door, not sure how she'd get inside. She rang the doorbell and knocked loudly a few times just to make sure she wouldn't be walking in on anyone, but no one answered.

She should stop. Go back. It wasn't too late.

For half a second, she convinced herself that was the right thing to do, but in her heart, she knew there could be no turning back.

She lifted her hand to test the doorknob. A loud hiss erupted from the trees, and she froze. She turned slowly, expecting some airborne hex to come flying her way and chop off her head or shoot her in the heart. She should have figured Glenys would set a ward to be sure no one could waltz right into her private space.

Instead, she found a fat ginger cat stalking her way, and she lost it. "*Are you crazy?* What are you doing here? You nearly scared me to death, and I don't have nine lives like you."

Mr. Kitty strolled from the trees as if he was out for a casual afternoon walk. Instead of approaching her, he headed down the drive, past where she'd left her bike, and disappeared.

"*Aargh!*" He would literally be the death of her.

She gave the doorknob one more glance and then hurried to follow him. A quaint white gazebo sat in the back corner of Glenys' yard, beneath a canopy of trees. She counted five herb gardens flourishing back there with all shades of green leaves and several with purple or white tiny flowers.

But that darned cat was nowhere in sight.

A sinking feeling descended upon her. He wouldn't...trick her, would he? Play a practical joke? He wouldn't tell her to secure an ancient book to her stomach, peddle across town, and then laugh as he watched her try to break into the house of the most powerful witch in town.

She had been foul-tempered with him a few times, but—

A loud click came from the direction of the backdoor, and she shifted her gaze there. The noise sounded an awful lot like a lock disengaging. She couldn't string words together that might explain what she already knew.

To prove it, she strode to the backdoor and turned the handle. Inside, she found a sassy ginger cat sitting by the polished, cherrywood kitchen table with a smirk on his face. She snorted in disbelief. "I don't want to know how you did that." Okay, maybe she did, but...

She closed the door behind her and turned to him. "If you're so smart, now what?"

He dropped his gaze to her stomach, and she realized the book had grown warm against her skin. A buzzing began in her ears, and she looked around the charming room with its intricate crown moulding, moss green walls and sheer ivory curtains for the source.

Mr. Kitty straightened his tail and crossed the hardwood floors toward the hallway. At this point, she'd be silly not to follow. Her cat might drive her insane, but he'd never steered her wrong when it came to serious stuff. She hoped.

At the end of the hall, just off a small bedroom decorated with a green and brown Boho feel, he stopped. He sat and glanced up at her expectantly.

Clarabelle's book vibrated with the same intensity as the noise in her ears. "It's here. Isn't it?" she whispered. "Glenys' book."

He lifted his chin in an affirmative gesture.

But where? She searched the creamy walls, wooden floors and mouldings, but nothing stood out. She took a few backward steps and noticed the humming dropped slightly. Forward, it increased.

The spell book was a darned homing device for the other tome.

She dropped to her knees near the opened bedroom doorway and searched in earnest, looking at each crack between the floorboards, along the mouldings, and then into the bedroom doorway.

Near the bottom of the doorframe was the tiniest crack. The tome next to her stomach buzzed like a thousand bees. *Holy harpies.*

Her fingernail barely fit into the gap, and she wrenched it toward her. The painted piece of wood fell into her hand. Her heart thundered, and she glanced into the narrow space.

A small book, covered in red leather, waited like a newly-discovered opal amidst handfuls of clear quartz. She reached for it and pulled it free from its hiding space.

The tome wasn't the same as her grandmother's but similar.

Mr. Kitty meowed his approval, and she spared him a glance. "Thank you, kind sir."

For the first time ever, he purred, and she nearly fell back on her bottom in surprise. She smiled and cracked open the book, flipping to the last pages where she'd found the dark spells in her grandmother's book.

As she searched, an eerie sensation slithered around her, and she shivered.

Then she found it. "*Obliteration,*" she whispered. This had to be it.

A loud crack of thunder ripped through the air startling her. Rain hit the roof overhead, the drops of water sounding more like a spattering of pebbles.

She'd seen this spell in Clarabelle's book but hadn't realized they'd meant to use it against the whole town. That was some crazy thinking, and now Glenys wanted to do the same?

She located the same spell in her grandmother's book and compared the two. Some of the components were the same as Clarabelle's, but others had been written where there had been blank spaces in her book. Several that Clarabelle had were missing from this one.

Glenys' book also appeared to have the second half of the spell, and Hazel wondered if there were more than two books with information. Though Glenys had mentioned she'd love to find Clarabelle's book, so maybe they were the only ones.

Either way, Charlie had been correct in what Belinda had told him. If Glenys was ever able to possess Clarabelle's book, she would have the capability to destroy the town, and she would have killed Belinda to keep her plan a secret.

Now what?

This time, she did sit back until her bottom hit the floor. She needed to find a way to tell Peter.

But short of Glenys confessing, Hazel couldn't see any possible way to make her pay for her crime. And she highly doubted Glenys would say a word...

Unless she was forced to confess.

Clarabelle's truth-telling spell.

The answer to her question sat closer to her heart than she ever expected. Pulling off the spell without tipping off a super powerful witch might be more than she could handle.

But she had to try.

CHAPTER TWENTY-TWO

Hazel pedaled straight into town, the wheels of her bike coasting over wet streets. The rain stopped as abruptly as it had started, though the ominously dark skies threatened more. The air was alive with electric tension and smells of Mother Earth. She inhaled deeply, letting it fuel her intentions.

She parked her bike against the brick wall outside Cora's Café. She put on her brightest smile before she opened the door and walked in. The restaurant was buzzing with customers in for the Tuesday fried egg and ham special, and it took Hazel a few seconds to find Cora helping customers at the far end of the café. Though her heart flopped like a fish on land, she waited patiently for her friend to finish and make her way back to the counter.

"Hi," she said as Cora approached. "Sorry to bail this morning."

Cora shook off her apology with a shake of her head. "Everything okay?"

Hazel sighed. "Yeah, just a personal issue."

Cora gave her a knowing "oh", and Hazel let her assume what she would.

"Hey, I need to stop by the bank this morning and wanted to take Glenys her favorite morning drink as a friendly gesture. Do you know what she likes?"

Cora leaned closer to Hazel. "Planning to check her out?" she whispered.

Hazel lifted a shoulder and let it drop. "I do need to take in my loan application for the old house on Hemlock, but..." She gave her a sly smile. She couldn't very well say she wasn't going to ask Glenys anything, but she didn't want to draw attention to her actions.

That information brought a smile to Cora's face. "Oooh, the Hemlock house. You're finally going to buy it."

"Yeah," she said thoughtfully. "I really love it."

"Awesome, and yeah, I know what Glenys likes to drink." She snorted. "Sorry that it's not any of your teas."

Hazel shook her head and smiled. "I just have to accept that not everyone is as smart as we are."

Cora laughed. "That's right. Give me just a second to get it for you."

Her friend didn't question her further when she gave her the coffee, and Hazel headed out into the forebodingly overcast day.

Hazel's pulse continued to hum as she stepped inside the bank, but from fear this time instead of from the spell books.

Glenys came out to greet her dressed in a slim-fitting black skirt and jacket, wearing a friendly smile on her face. Hazel opened her senses, searching for the warmth from her previous visit. It was there, but when she dug deeper, she found holes where there shouldn't have been any.

"Good to see you again, Hazel. Sorry that I still haven't made it into your teashop. After Grant's death, I haven't been very social."

"I understand." She gave her a no-worries smile and held the coffee toward her. "I hear you like coffee better, anyway. Fresh cup straight from Cora's, just the way you like."

"How nice." Glenys eyed the cup with pleasure. "I guess this means we're still friends despite the coffee-tea thing."

Hazel snorted. "Of course. Hey, I stopped by to drop off my loan papers, but I also need to speak with you for a minute." She held out the application as proof.

Glenys took the signed document and placed it on Lachlan's desk as they passed. Inside her office, she closed the door behind them.

"You seem to be full of energy today. How are things going for you?" Glenys asked.

She hadn't thought that Glenys might sense the tomes now hiding in her bag. "I'm great. You?" If Glenys detected her own spell book, Hazel didn't know what she'd do.

"Perfectly awesome. Thank you so much for helping to put Timothy behind bars. I've felt much safer since then."

She wouldn't if she knew how easy it had been for Mr. Kitty to break into her house.

Glenys slid into the chair behind her desk. "I know it won't be permanent until after the trial, but I have faith he'll be locked away forever."

Hazel sat and waited for Glenys to take a drink before she pressed forward, hoping her words would mask any odd taste. "That's actually the other part of the reason I'm here. Peter needs to talk to you."

Glenys seemed shocked. "To me? Why?" She frowned and took another sip.

Hazel released a weighted sigh. Here goes nothing. "I gave him the document you gave me, but he said they wouldn't be able to use it in court without your presence. Something about the person bringing forth the evidence needed to be present, or it wouldn't be admissible. I knew you were desperate to have Timothy behind bars, so I eventually told Peter it was you."

Glenys' features hardened, and displeasure radiated from her. "I thought I made it clear that I couldn't have my name involved."

Hazel widened her eyes in innocence. "Yes, I know, but Peter promised he wouldn't bring you into this at all until he talks to you. He's a very discreet man, so you don't have to worry."

She snorted. "Unless he belongs to the other team."

Hazel shook her head, keeping an earnest gaze locked on Glenys. "I'm positive he doesn't." Though she wished she really could be that certain.

"Just a short, five-minute conversation," Hazel continued. "In fact, we could go right now if you're able to get away. I don't know how particular your boss is about you coming and going as you please." She prayed pushing that ego button would help get her moving.

"Of course, I can leave when I want. I'm the bank manager."

Uh-huh. Hazel held up her hands in a sign of calming peace. "A few minutes is all it will take to clear this up, and Peter can tell you directly what your options are as far as coming forward. Maybe he will know a way you can worm out of going to court." With her personality, that also ought to tempt Glenys.

"But it's raining, and I paid a lot for this suit."

"No, it stopped a few minutes ago. If we go now, we should be good."

"Okay, fine." She opened her drawer, removed her purse, and stood. "Let's fix your ridiculous blunder."

Hazel wanted to say that the only blunder had been Glenys thinking she could get away with murder. "Wonderful. Why don't you bring your coffee? Maybe it will help ease my stupid mistake."

Glenys gave her a nasty smirk. "Maybe so."

As they left the bank, Hazel offered a silent prayer to the Blessed Mother, hoping she hadn't screwed up the truth-telling spell and that Glenys had drunk enough of her spiked coffee for it to work. If Hazel recalled correctly, she hadn't had to wait long for it to work when she'd tried it on herself.

Margaret seemed surprised when Hazel walked in with Glenys in tow. "Morning, ladies." She flicked her gaze between the two of them.

"Hi, Margaret. Is Peter available? It's important we talk to him this morning."

Instead of sending Hazel back as usual, she stood. "Let me check."

Hazel's heart thundered as Margaret strode to Peter's office, her bright green tulle skirt swishing as she walked.

There were so many ways this could go wrong. Glenys' annoyance rolled off her in waves, multiplying her anxiety.

Margaret walked back with a smile. "He's available. Go ahead and go in."

Glenys' heels clicked smartly as they crossed the reception area to his office. Hazel stepped in first and gave him what she hoped was a heads-up smile.

Peter stood and welcomed them to have a seat with a gesture of his hand and then he closed his office door. "What can I help you with?"

Hazel barely let him finish his sentence before she replied. "Glenys is here to talk about the document I gave you, the one with Timothy's signature."

"Yes," Glenys interjected. "I don't understand why I have to be present when the evidence is introduced in court."

Peter focused on Hazel with the smallest telltale sign of confusion in his gaze. "Well, Glenys, having you in court and being able to say how you acquired the evidence gives it more legitimacy."

Hazel fought to keep her relief from showing as she gave thanks for Peter's brilliant mind.

Glenys shot Hazel with a glare. "What if I refuse?"

Peter shrugged. "We could subpoena you."

Angry tension erupted in the room. "You don't understand. This could ruin my reputation," Glenys said.

"Maybe you could tell us how you ended up with it?" Hazel suggested, needing to test her spell.

"I stole it." Glenys' expertly-outlined eyes grew wide in horror. She turned to Hazel, her features blasting fear. *"You didn't."*

This was it. The moment she could push forward and make Glenys confess, potentially exposing her own heritage to others. Or she could choose to let it go, move back home, and pretend everything she'd learned and experienced in Stonebridge had never happened. And hope that Glenys didn't hunt her down and sacrifice her.

Blessed Mother, how she wished she could choose the latter. She shivered as though frozen to the bone. She had to do this.

"I think you know more about Belinda's death than you're saying, don't you?"

CHAPTER TWENTY-THREE

Yes." The answer to Hazel's question shot from Glenys' mouth. Color drained from her face, and she stood. Her gaze darted toward the door.

Before she could make her escape, Hazel jumped to her feet and blocked the way. Glenys snarled and, without warning, charged Hazel. She caught her around the midriff and tackled her to the floor.

Harsh, angry whispers rushed from Glenys' mouth, and the protective medallion Cora had given her heated and singed her neck. Curses, Hazel realized. Deep in the throes of fear, Hazel scrambled, trying to get free from Glenys' pummeling fists.

Then suddenly, Glenys magically lifted from her body. She screamed and flailed as Peter hauled her backward. More curses poured from Glenys' mouth. Peter let out a surprised grunt, and his face grew red, though Hazel couldn't see what Glenys had done to him.

She jumped to her feet and rushed toward the struggling couple. Peter managed to keep her in a tight hold despite shaking muscles and sweat dripping down his face. Instinctively, she covered Glenys' mouth with her hand, stopping Glenys' angry spells aimed at him.

Glenys struggled to bite her, and Hazel relinquished her hold when she nipped the underside of her forefinger.

"Stop it, Glenys," she yelled. "It's too late! You're caught."

Glenys panted. "You can't stop me." She started another string of ancient-sounding words.

Hazel glanced frantically about the area, searching for anything that she could use as a gag. She swiped a paper from Peter's desk and shoved it into Glenys' mouth. The more Glenys cursed and struggled to speak, the more Hazel stuffed it between her lips, until Glenys could only mumble.

She tried to spit out the wad, but Hazel held it in place.

A rapid knock sounded at the door, and Margaret thrust it open. "Is everything—"

She paused as though stunned, her gaze jumping to each person in the room.

Glenys moaned against Hazel's hand and struggled to free herself from Peter's grip.

"Tape," Peter demanded in a breathy voice.

Margaret hurried forward and ripped off a long piece. Hazel released Glenys long enough to run it from cheek to cheek. Margaret and Hazel repeated the procedure, securing more pieces of tape until Glenys' face looked like a badly wrapped package.

Hazel stepped back, panting and grateful that Glenys was unable to cast a spell with her glaring eyes.

Margaret glanced at her boss as though he'd gone insane. "What on earth?"

The warning in his expression would terrify most. "*Hazel. Handcuffs*. In my top drawer."

He turned to Margaret. "Go out and keep everyone away from my door. Please. I don't need the whole office to hear this, especially the feds, until I know what's going on."

Margaret gave a swift nod, her skirt rustling as she hurried away. "I've got your back," she called. She closed the door behind her, and Hazel could hear her talking to others, calming them.

Hazel procured the cuffs, and Peter slapped them on Glenys and then forced her into one of his chairs.

He rounded on Hazel. "What in the hell is this all about?"

Her breaths came short and fast. She didn't know what to do or say. She couldn't make Glenys confess if every other word she spoke could curse them. But she couldn't allow Peter to release her, either. "I think she killed Belinda. She's here to confess."

Glenys did her best to scream her disagreement from behind the layers of tape.

Peter's body was rigid, most likely full of adrenaline like hers, and he was angry. So angry. "That's not how it appears."

Hazel's ire jumped into the fray. She would not bring things this far and then fail. "Fine. Let me rephrase. Glenys has a lot of information she's withheld from the police regarding Belinda's murder." She shot an angry look at Glenys. "Isn't that right?"

Her eyes darkened with fury, but she nodded.

Peter's expression grew curious. "You have further information you'd like to tell me?" he asked Glenys.

Glenys shook her head.

Peter growled in frustration and stared down Hazel, showing her he'd lost his patience. "Again, I'll ask...what the hell is going on?"

Hazel was in way over her head, and her instincts screamed for her to run. She sucked in air and tried to calm her shaking.

She knew she'd have a lot to explain after everything was said and done. But right now, she couldn't let Glenys go free. "You're not asking her correctly. You have to be more direct."

Peter snorted in disbelief. "You're kidding."

She shook her head.

His look promised her suggestion had better deliver or else. He scrubbed his chin as he turned from Hazel to Glenys.

The look in Glenys' eyes morphed from wrath to panic.

He studied Glenys for several moments. "Okay, then. I'll play along with this ridiculous...whatever it is and head straight for the heart of it. Did you, Glenys Everwood kill Belinda Atkins?"

Glenys' eyes bugged, and she convulsed. Hazel was sure she'd combust from the inside out as she obviously struggled not to answer. Then slowly, her head bobbed up and down.

Peter widened his eyes as though amazed. "I'll be a donkey's behind. You killed Belinda."

Glenys nodded again and then speared Hazel with a look that promised she'd make Hazel pay for her treachery.

Peter approached Glenys and lifted his hand as though to remove the tape.

"*Don't,*" Hazel cried. "She'll..." Oh Blessed Mother, help her. "She'll be able to curse you if you do."

He looked at her as if she was an imbecile. "I'm not afraid of a little swearing."

She held a hand up and stepped closer to stop him physically if necessary. "No. I mean she'll cast a curse upon you."

That stopped him cold. Fear flickered in his eyes. "Then what exactly would you like me to do with her? In order to arrest her, I'll need to interrogate. Can't very well do that with tape over her mouth."

"I'm not sure." Crap. She hadn't thought this out. Someone must know that answer. Not her mother. Maybe Cora? "Can you give me a few minutes to make a phone call?"

He folded his arms in front of him, and the action caused his biceps to stretch the brown fabric of his uniform. "Sure. Why not?" His words were innocuous enough, but anger and frustration simmered behind them nonetheless.

Feeling the venomous stare from Glenys and the irritated one from Peter, she slipped the phone from her pocket and dialed Cora. She prayed her actions weren't somehow putting her friend at risk.

"Hi," she said, purposefully not mentioning her name. "You're not going to believe this, but I've discovered the killer, and I'm in a bit of a bind. The person will confess if prompted, but there's also a high probability she'll hex us, too."

Cora's gasped came across the line, followed by a long trail of silence. "Are you serious?"

Hazel swallowed. "Very. I need to know if there's a way subdue someone's powers that will still allow that person to talk."

"You're not going to tell me who it is?"

"I'm not in a position to do that right now. I just need to know if there's a spell that will work." If not, she had no idea how to get out of this tangle.

"Oh, sugar. I don't know." A long pause stretched between them as she thought. "Glenys might be able to consult her grandmother's spell book. There could be something there."

She exhaled, feeling the beckoning of the two tomes in her bag. "That's a great idea. Thanks." She ended the call and turned to Peter. "Do you mind if I take a quick bathroom break?"

His eyebrows shot upward. "Now?"

She picked up her purse and headed toward the door. "I'll just be a minute." She rushed from his office and headed to the public bathroom where she barricaded herself in a stall.

What had she been thinking? Any fool could have planned this better.

Her hands shook as she pulled Clarabelle's tome from her purse. She'd start there. Since it belonged to her family, and technically now her, it might be inclined to reveal its secrets to her quicker.

She pictured Mr. Kitty shaking his head in admonition because she hadn't studied it all the times he'd forced it in front of her.

Hazel held the book close to her chest and closed her eyes. She whispered a quick prayer to the Blessed Mother to help her find what she needed. Faking confidence, she opened her eyes, ran her finger along the edge of the pages. When a touch of energy zinged her, she opened the book.

Halfway down the page, the words Suppress and Subdue jumped out at her. The Blessed Mother, Clarabelle, or the Fates had come through for her.

She would need to place a drop of blood on a brass pendant and press it against Glenys' neck whilst repeating "thou shall do no harm" three times. This would supposedly suppress her abilities for one hour.

Frustration threatened to break her. She didn't have a brass pendant. Wasn't even sure where she might locate one. But she was in so far that she couldn't back out now.

If Peter was unable to get a signed confession, he'd have to release Glenys. And Hazel had no doubt that the second that tape was off her mouth, she'd turn Hazel, Peter, and likely Margaret to ash.

The idea of returning to Peter's office and telling him that she'd managed to locate a spell that might help them, but she didn't have all the necessary components was ludicrous. Asking him to read Glenys her rights and lock her up for several hours so Hazel could locate a brass pendant would not go over well. The feds would surely catch wind of that.

Peter wouldn't be able to explain the situation without losing his job. He'd be laughed at, and his reputation would be destroyed.

She exited the bathroom and tried to swallow past the hardened lump of fear and regret that choked her. She had to think of something—

An officer walked in her path, and her heart leapt. The gun at his hip reminded her of the time Peter had showed her his gun and explained the process of firing a bullet...*from a brass casing.*

She strode as fast as she could without generating notice, back to his office.

CHAPTER TWENTY-FOUR

Inside the police chief's office, Hazel closed the door behind her. Peter waited with an expectant look while Glenys glared. "I have it figured out. I need one of your bullets and string of any kind. I need something sharp, too."

Glenys mumbled in protest and tried to stand.

Peter pushed her back into the chair. Suspicion radiated from him. "I don't have any string."

Hazel glanced wildly about his office and spied a container of paper clips on his desk. "Those will do." She hoped.

She quickly linked paper clips together until they formed a chain. She held out her hand. "Bullet."

He hesitated. "What do you intend to do with it?"

She didn't have time to explain everything to him. He wouldn't understand anyway. "I don't actually need a bullet. Just the brass. So, unless you have a brass pendant lying around..." She shoved her hand out farther.

Resigned, he slipped his gun from the holster, removed a bullet, and held it over her hand. "I need to know where you're going with this. This whole thing is pushing the boundaries of acceptable police conduct, not to mention social norms."

She met his gaze and held it. "Do you trust me, Peter?"

He hesitated and then sighed. "I do." The bullet landed in her palm, and she closed her hand around it.

After a little finagling, she had herself a fine-looking brass pendant. Or at least one that would do the job.

She scanned his office again. "Something sharp?" Before he could respond, she pointed to a push pin on a bulletin board. She snatched it and turned to Glenys. She didn't think the book had specified whose blood she needed, but she wasn't taking chances.

She approached Glenys who wriggled and flung herself forward to escape Hazel.

Peter jerked her back into the chair, held her steady, and caught Hazel with a pained expression. "Tell me this isn't happening."

She pushed away the anguish that reached out to her. She couldn't think about Peter or what she'd just done to their relationship. She had to focus on the spell or she'd surely mess up again.

"Sorry, not sorry," she said to Glenys and pricked her thigh.

Glenys screamed behind the tape and a drop of blood welled on the surface. Hazel rubbed the bullet across it, and then secured the makeshift pendant around Glenys' neck.

"This is beyond unorthodox," Peter muttered.

"I know," she whispered.

Glenys kicked hard, catching her in the shin, and she cried out.

In the end, her actions only furthered Hazel's resolve. If the witch thought she could intimidate her, she could think again. Hazel shot her a parting look and closed her eyes. She repeated the spell three times, invoking Mother Earth's energy to keep Glenys from harming them.

When she finished, she opened her eyes to find Glenys staring hard.

Peter's face had turned ashen. "What was that?"

The look of disbelief and fear in his eyes nearly destroyed her. If there had ever been a chance for her and Peter, she'd eviscerated it.

Instead of answering him, she ripped the tape off Glenys' mouth, the sound bringing her satisfaction if not solace. "You can question her now. You have an hour before this wears off, at which time I highly recommend you gag her again. Don't waste any time."

Glenys growled. "You'll pay for this."

Hazel met her gaze and sighed. "You can't hurt me now."

A twinkle of danger danced in her eyes. "There's always later, witch."

Peter pulled Glenys from the chair and led her toward the door. He opened it and then glanced back. "Stay here. When I'm finished with Glenys, I'll be back for you." He shut the door with a firm thud.

She placed her hand over her mouth and broke. Soul-deep emotion sprang to the surface like angry welts after a beating. She'd brought Belinda's killer to justice and had destroyed every good thing in her life in the process.

She'd just practiced witchcraft in front of the police chief in a town that was known to viciously punish people for such acts. If she was lucky, Peter would tell her to get lost and never look at her again.

If she wasn't... She couldn't bear to go there right now.

She knew one thing though. She wasn't about to sit and wait for Peter to break her heart and bring justice down on her head. Or for someone to tell Officer John Bartles she was a witch. She grabbed tissues and strode out of his office, not pausing when Margaret called after her.

If she was smart, she'd head home and pack up everything. She'd never speak a word to anyone about what had just taken place in Peter's office. But life wasn't that easy, and she'd already determined she was a few twigs short of a full broom.

If she kept this all inside her, she'd wither from the worry, pain and ugliness. So, instead of going home, she walked her bike to Cora's.

Cora looked up from a nearby table where she chatted with some locals and recoiled. She held up a finger indicating she needed a moment. Hazel sank to the bench for waiting customers, and a few minutes later, Cora reappeared minus her apron. She wrapped a hand around Hazel's arm. "Let's walk."

Hazel did her best to stifle her sobs as Cora led them on their usual walking trail until they reached the solace of the park. Instead of crossing the small bridge, they headed across the grass to a bench where Hazel dropped and buried her face in her hands.

Cora wrapped an arm across her shoulders and squeezed. "You're not okay. What on earth has happened?"

Hazel wiped her tears with a wad of tissues and tried to breathe through the anguish. "I ruined everything."

Cora drew her brows together. "How?"

Genuine warmth and empathy rushed from her friend and into her soul, and she accepted its strength. "Glenys killed Belinda."

Pain contorted Cora's features. "*No...*" The word erupted as a breathless wail. "How could she be so cruel? Belinda didn't deserve that."

Hazel met her friend's tear-filled gaze and hugged her. "I'm so sorry."

"She... I..." Cora shook her head, unable to find the words she needed.

"It's worse." Hazel inhaled a shaky breath. "I used a truth-telling spell before we went to Peter's office, not realizing that if she could talk to tell the truth, she could also curse us."

Cora gripped her tighter. "*Hazel...*"

Her friend's reaction made her feel as though she'd signed her own death warrant. Maybe she had. "I had to cast a spell to keep her from practicing magic while in custody. He's getting a confession out of her now."

"But then what?" Cora seemed more concerned than ever. "Once that wears off, he won't be able to keep her in check."

"He can gag her again."

"*Forever?* You know that's not possible."

Tangled emotions broke her, and she sobbed. "I don't know, Cora. I don't know what to do. I never should have messed with things I don't know about or understand." She struggled to inhale. "I only wanted to help."

Cora wiped her tears. "You did help, Hazel. You did. You were brave, and now I'm going to have to be brave, too."

Hazel sniffed and shook her head in confusion. "How?"

"I'll call the authorities."

"That won't do any good. Federal agents are already stationed in Peter's office."

"Not those authorities. There's a special unit who works for the government. Most of us would never want to engage them or draw attention to ourselves, but we have no choice. Glenys cannot be allowed to hurt anyone again, and they could never keep her in a regular jail."

Hazel struggled to comprehend. She'd never heard of a governmental entity who handled bad witches. "How do we let them know about her?"

"This part is on me. Don't you worry. You've put yourself in enough danger. I'll take care of this. The less you know, the better. Trust me."

She nodded, wishing she could feel reassured by Cora's words. "What do I do about Peter?" she whispered. "Do you think I'm safe in Stonebridge?"

Cora took her hand. "I don't think he'd do anything to hurt you. He's not that type of person."

Hazel's heart trembled. "He said witches don't belong here."

Cora gave her a shrug filled with attitude and wiped her tears. "I guess he'll have to get over that then, won't he?"

She gave her a watery smile even though she didn't believe for a second that Peter would. "Thank you for loaning me your medallion. I think it saved our lives." She pulled it from beneath her shirt and over her head to return it.

"Oh..." Cora widened her eyes. "I'm so glad to hear that, but you keep it until you increase the strength of your magic."

She didn't know what she'd done to deserve Cora. "You're a good friend. Will you let me know what happens with Glenys?"

"You betcha. Go home and rest. I'll check in with you later."

They both stood and walked solemnly back to the center of town. Cora hugged her before she headed into her café. Hazel checked to make sure Gretta was okay to stay in the shop all day before she climbed on her bike and pedaled home.

She had a raging headache, two magical tomes in her bag that she needed to hide, and a cat to thank for his help.

EPILOGUE

A soft spring breeze ruffled Hazel's hair as she pulled weeds from an overgrown garden along the back of Clarabelle's old home. The loan she'd applied for hadn't gone through yet and might not for some time since she was sure everything at the bank was in chaos after Glenys' arrest.

That didn't mean she couldn't care for a place that had once belonged to her family. Lavender, sage and nightshade fought for space amongst the weeds, and Hazel wondered if what she saw before her might be offspring from something Clarabelle had planted long ago.

A soft caress touched her cheek, and she paused to smile. Clarabelle was there, letting her know she approved of Hazel's service.

Mr. Kitty watched her from a sunny spot across the lawn, his eyes droopy with sleep. Maybe later, she'd stretch out on the grass and nap with him. She doubted anyone would enter the property and catch her back there.

Two weeks had passed since the whole incident. She hadn't seen nor heard from Peter. She hoped that meant he'd leave her in peace. It would take her a long while to get over him, but they'd never been meant for each other, and one day, she'd find a way to be happy again.

Of course, her heart didn't believe that, but she'd have to rely on her brains for a while.

If she ever was lucky enough to own this place, she'd need to hire Charlie again to help her with the overgrown trees and shrubs. Or maybe she'd leave it. She kind of liked the wildness of it.

Mr. Kitty's sudden dash into the trees startled her, and she whipped around, alert for danger.

Peter stood not far from her, near the edge of the property that butted up against the magical grove of trees with his hands buried deep in the pockets of his jeans. She got to her feet, putting her in a less vulnerable position. They both stared for several long moments. Hazel opened her senses, looking for malice or any other hint as to Peter's intentions.

Nothing.

Her heart pulsed in sickening thumps. "Are you here to arrest me? To turn me in for being a witch?"

He shook his head but didn't speak.

She swallowed. "Then why are you here?"

He shrugged.

Another bout of silence stretched between them. Her heart begged her to make amends while her mind argued it was a lost cause. "I never wanted to lie to you."

His stoic expression didn't change. "Then why did you?"

Her composure broke. "Because of this town, the way everyone is against witches, including you. I wanted to be here, to learn more about my heritage and what happened so long ago, but people wouldn't let me. Not if they knew."

After several long seconds, he gave a quick nod. "Just so you know, at the end of Glenys' questioning before the feds sedated her, she called out you and many others, labeling you as the damned."

Hazel inhaled. For all she knew, someone could be plotting against her right now.

"I don't think anyone believed her," he continued. "She named too many people and was out of her mind with rage. The men who took her said it was unlikely she'd be fit for trial. She'll end up in a mental institution."

For witches.

"How many people?" she asked quietly. She'd like to know who amongst the town might be an ally.

He gave a dubious snort. "I think you already know."

"I don't, though. I'm new here, remember? Besides Belinda and Glenys, I only know of one other person."

He shook his head, dismissing her question. "Others can tell you. I'm not one to speculate and spread rumors."

Of course. As police chief, he wouldn't. He was right though. She'd hear it from others.

She accepted his statement with a nod. "Did she say why she killed Belinda? I've only been able to guess at it. And what about Grant? Did she murder him, too?"

"Whatever you did to her made her spill everything. I wish all suspects were so forthcoming."

If he'd truly let her, she might be able to help him with that. But then that would put him in danger, too.

He kicked at a clod of dirt on the grass. "Glenys had thought Belinda had the potential and lineage to be more powerful than her. Supposedly a descendant of one of the original four. If she couldn't lie, then I suppose that was true."

A shiver raced over Hazel. "Did she say which one?"

His gaze hardened. "No, and I didn't ask."

She nodded solemnly. "Of course." He wouldn't want to know.

"She gloated about hatching what should have been the perfect murder that would take out two foes at once, Belinda and Timothy. She probably would have gotten away with it if not for you."

Hazel wanted to feel proud of that, but she only felt sick. "I wasn't trying to take her down. I just wanted to find Belinda's killer and help Cora with closure."

"I guess you can't help but be a good detective. Did you use a scrying mirror or something similar?"

Hazel frowned. "No. I don't own such a thing."

"Then how did you figure it out?"

She shrugged, trying not to feel insulted. "Same way you would have, by following the clues and asking questions."

He seemed doubtful, and it broke her heart that she'd lost his trust. But what could she expect. She'd have to settle with being grateful he wouldn't persecute her.

"Thanks for the heads-up that she named me. I appreciate it." Though in his eyes, she probably didn't deserve it. Maybe it was a parting gift for what would never be.

She focused on the garden and blinked rapidly, willing her tears to remain hidden. She knelt and buried her hand-shovel to the hilt into the rich dirt, letting him know she was finished with their conversation. There was no need to continue. They would go on with their lives, and she would do her best to survive this.

"Hazel."

She glanced up, surprised to find him walking toward her. "I thought you were leaving."

He clenched his jaw. "Is that what you want? You want me to leave and pretend there was never anything between us?"

Tears slipped from her eyes. "No, of course not. But I can't picture any scenario where you'd want to stay."

He held out a hand. She accepted it, and he pulled her to her feet. "My feelings don't turn off like that. Trust me, I've tried."

"I wouldn't blame you if you did."

"Yeah? Well, it's not that easy. Whatever was between us felt real. At least to me."

She pulled off her garden gloves and let them fall to the ground. "For me, too. But it could never work. Not when you don't believe witches should live here. I should never have let you kiss me that first time."

"Are you serious?"

"If I hadn't, I wouldn't be hurting you this way." She placed a hand over her chest. "I literally feel it right here, and I hate myself for doing that to you."

He glanced at her hand and then to her face. His beautiful green eyes bored into hers for a very long time. "Are you planning to leave Stonebridge?"

She shook her head. "I probably should for safety reasons, but I've already put earnest money down on this house. I want to buy it and live here." She swore she could hear his heart thundering in sync with hers.

"If you stay, you'll have me and my department working to keep you safe."

The spark of hope he gave her exploded. "But I'm a witch."

"Trust me. I'm well aware of that fact."

She wanted to reach out to him, to touch his cheek, but she didn't dare. "Are you asking me to stay?"

"Yes, Hazel," he said without hesitation. "I'm asking you to stay. I don't know how we'll make things work, but you're in my heart, and I don't want to think of a future without you."

He opened his arms.

"Then I'll stay." She stepped into his embrace, burying her face against his neck. The scent of his cologne and the sound of his heart would always feel like home to her.

She had no idea how they'd make things work, but she knew she wanted to try. "I should warn you. One of my ancestors haunts this house. She can get a little moody at times, but she's nice."

A low chuckle rumbled from his chest. "You mean Clarabelle? Don't worry. She likes me."

Bewildered, she leaned back to look into his eyes.

"What?" he shrugged. "It's a police chief's duty to keep an eye on things. I've had to chase kids off this property more than a few times. She's let me know she's grateful."

Hazel gave a soft snort of amazement. "You should probably kiss me before I start thinking about this too much and my head explodes."

His smile deepened, putting her world back into alignment. "I'm under your spell. How could I refuse?"

His lips captured hers in a heart-melting kiss, and for a moment, she had no worries what tomorrow would bring. Everything that mattered was right here, right now.

* * *

If you enjoyed reading this book, the greatest gift you can give me is to leave a review at Amazon or Goodreads and tell a friend. It helps others find stories they might love and motivates me to keep writing.

Thank you and happy reading,
Cindy

****

Read on for an excerpt from Book Four in the Teas and Temptations Cozy Mystery Series, Four Warned.

Excerpt from FOUR WARNED

Teas and Temptations Cozy Mystery Series
Book Four

Hazel consulted the gadget on her wrist and then sent an annoyed look in Cora's direction. "I feel like a dog."

Cora turned a curiously disturbed look in her direction. "Huh?"

"I have to walk to get my treats. We've been out for nearly an hour, and I've only burned enough for one and a half cherry macaroons. Why is life so cruel?" Not to mention, the sun seemed extra hot today even though it was barely past ten a.m.

Cora snickered as she pumped her elbows to increase her workout. "Hasn't anyone told you, life isn't fair?"

"Well, it should be. If I get the chance, I'll be talking to the Blessed Mother about that one."

Cora grinned. "You do that. Just make sure it's not until you're really old."

"Then what's the point?" she said sarcastically. "If I'm ready to leave Earth, then it won't matter. I need someone to fix this now."

Her friend chuckled as they turned onto Camden Street. "Good luck with that one."

Hazel spied several people gathered on the church's lawn ahead and narrowed her gaze to see better. "What's going on at the old church?"

"Not sure," Cora said. "Let's find out."

As they neared, Hazel spotted the church's priest outside with Lobster Lucy standing next to a folding table and Mrs. Tillens seated on the only chair. She'd never had the unfortunate pleasure of meeting the priest, and instinct told her she didn't want to now.

Hazel slowed her stride. "Let's turn around."

Cora drew her brows together. "Why?"

"The priest is there, and I really don't want to be anywhere near him."

"Father Christopher?" She shrugged. "He's all right."

That didn't help her anxiety in the least. "He freaks me out. I'm afraid he's going to sense my magic, or the church will crumble if I go anywhere near it." It wasn't that she had an aversion to churches, just *this* church.

Cora's chuckle echoed through the stifling morning air.

Hazel came to a complete stop and turned her back to the church. "I'm serious. I get bad vibes from him."

"He's just a regular man, Hazel. He can't sense magic or read auras. If he did, they'd kick him out of the church."

"Maybe so, but don't forget Timothy Franklin has magic in his blood even though he doesn't claim it, and he secretly uses it against us. So, maybe the priest does, too, and we don't know it."

Cora slipped her arm through Hazel's and turned her around. "Don't let them scare you. We have just as much right to be in this town as they do. Plus, we have skills they don't."

Just because they had a right, didn't mean they should tempt fate.

"Come meet him, and you'll see."

Curiosity and peer pressure fought her common sense and won. She allowed Cora to pull her along until they neared the lush grass, and then she slipped her arm free.

Father Christopher, Mrs. Tillens, and Lobster Lucy all looked up as she and Cora approached. When the priest locked his eyes on Hazel, she gave him a hesitant smile. The older man with thinning gray hair and a skeletal figure returned the gesture, but something about him gave her chills.

Lobster Lucy waved. "Cora. We were just talking about you." The older, larger woman looked as salty and sturdy as some of the crews who came in off the fishing boats when they were docked near town.

"Me?" Cora joined the group, while Hazel remained closer to the fringe. "What about me?"

Mrs. Tillens, with her silver hair looking freshly washed and coiffed, gave Hazel a small wave, and she returned it.

Lucy thumbed toward the priest. "Father Christopher hoped we'd have a lot more people enter this year for the May Day Chowder Chowdown. I told him that I bet if I could convince you to join the fray, more people would enter. A few of the jealous women in town have bragged that they can cook better than you. If you sign up, I'll tell them they have the chance to prove it or shut up."

Cora put a hand over her mouth as if to hide her surprise. "Oh, I don't know about competing. I've never been one to enjoy that."

Hazel watched the priest while he studied Cora.

"It's for a good cause," he said. "And it will help with some of those black marks you've gotten for not attending church." His chuckle came off as hollow.

Cora blushed. "Sorry, Father. I have been a little lax about attending."

Hazel was surprised to learn that Cora would step foot in a church that didn't accept her beliefs. Hazel would refuse. She might not freely admit she was a witch, but she wouldn't pretend to be something she wasn't, either.

"Is that your acceptance then?" he pushed. "With all the rumors around town, it will do a body good to let others know where your loyalties lie."

Hazel quelled a gasp at his veiled threat. Be seen at church, or be labeled a witch, especially now. Anti-witch anxieties in modern times had hit an all-time high recently after the circulating rumors about Glenys and her behavior before her recent arrest for murder. But to use that as a scare tactic was deplorable.

"Of course, Father. I'd love to help out." Cora's reply might have seemed enthusiastic, but Hazel sensed the churning beneath. It was very reminiscent of her own thoughts. She'd bet Cora wished she'd listened to her when she'd said they should turn around.

Mrs. Tillens' sweet smile grew wide. "How about you, Hazel, dear? Wouldn't you love to help us out, too?"

The priest and Lobster Lucy turned their gazes on her, and her mind went blank. She'd be having words with Cora later. "Umm...I'm not one who enjoys clam chowder, so that's probably a bad idea. I doubt mine would be edible."

Lucy waved away her concerns with an over-sized hand. "We don't just make chowder, Hazel. You can enter the bread or dessert category."

"We could even start a new category for drinks," Mrs. Tillens added enthusiastically. "You could bring tea."

Father Christopher nodded. "As long as it's not peanut tea."

Hazel gave him a quizzical look. She'd never heard of a tea made from peanuts. She lifted her hands in a hold-it-right-there gesture. "I'm sorry, but it's really not my thing."

"What's not your thing," John Bartles asked as he joined the group. His sandy blond hair looked freshly cut, and his eyes emitted the usual friendliness. He was an everyday, average kind of guy. At least on the outside.

Hazel grew leery. "Entering competitions."

The priest extended his hand. "Good to see you, Officer Bartles."

John shook it with familiar friendliness that left her anxious.

John turned back to her. "You're going to deny the church when they need you?"

"Come on, Hazel," Mrs. Tillens encouraged. "We have a lot of fun, and you might find new customers."

Apparently, her options came down to two things. She could refuse and draw the attention of the town's witch hunters, or keep the enemy in sight, but be a hypocrite. She pasted on her best fake smile. "I do have some teas that are lovely over ice. I think they'd go perfectly with clam chowder."

The clapped his hands together. "Wonderful. I love it when a town comes together and supports the church. We all need God in our lives, and what better way to do it."

She worked to keep a smile in place. She wouldn't argue that having a higher power in one's life was a good thing, but this was no leader or man of God standing before her. His aura was too dirty for that.

"Wonderful." Mrs. Tillens' face beamed with pleasure. "I don't know why I haven't invited you to church before now, Hazel. People would love you, and you'd fit in so well."

"That's very kind of you to say." Hazel shot a glance at Cora and hoped her friend realized they needed to leave before they had her signed up for a baptism. "What's the date?"

"Next Sunday," Lucy supplied. "I'll be baking my incredibly delicious strawberry tarts. I'll have a special one just for you Father Christopher."

Mrs. Tillens scoffed. "Now, now, Lucy. That sounds a little like cheating."

Lucy frowned. "Does not."

The older lady offered a polite smile. "You're showing the judge special treatment."

Lucy slid the strap of her overalls higher on her shoulder. "Anyone else can do the same. I think Father Christopher can retain his impartiality. Don't you, Father?"

All gazes slid to the priest.

He reassured them with a nod. "I always do my best to be a fair and honest judge."

"See?" Lucy said to Mrs. Tillens with a sizeable amount of snark in her voice.

Mrs. Tillens pursed her lips and turned her gaze toward the papers in front of her. She wouldn't argue, but she obviously didn't agree. "Hazel and Cora, would you please write your names and what you're bringing?"

Hazel begrudgingly took the pen she offered and signed up for the contest. She turned and handed the pen to Cora with a sugary, you're-going-to-pay-for-this smile.

If Cora thought her sheepish expression would earn her any favors, she was dead wrong.

Cora wrote her name and then handed the pen to John Bartles. "Is your wife bringing her amazing chocolate cake again this year?"

He grinned. "Absolutely. That's why I'm here."

Hazel wanted to be snide and ask him what he himself was bringing, not his wife, since he'd contributed to her being railroaded, but it was best to stay on his good side until she had proof he wasn't part of the Sons of Stonebridge that would love to run her out of town. If they let her live that long.

"Susan's cake is my favorite." Cora nudged Hazel with her elbow. "Wait until you taste it."

"I'm looking forward to it." Though Hazel doubted very much that it could compete with Cora's cherry macaroons. She caught Cora's attention. "We should probably get going. If I'm going to indulge in decadent chocolate cake, I'd better start burning more calories."

The group laughed.

Lucy stepped toward them. "I'll walk with you to the corner. See you later, John, Father Christopher." She didn't bother to say anything to Mrs. Tillens.

Hazel wanted to roll her eyes at their petty, small town drama but decided against it. She, apparently, was now one of the god-fearing citizens of Stonebridge. And everyone knew, good church-going people never acted that way.

She held back a snicker of laughter.

* * *

You can find FOUR WARNED, Teas and Temptations Cozy Mystery Series, Book Four, on Amazon.com.

Book List

TEAS & TEMPTATIONS COZY MYSTERIES (PG–Rated Fun):
Once Wicked
Twice Hexed
Three Times Charmed
Four Warned
The Fifth Curse
It's All Sixes
Spellbound Seven
Elemental Eight
Nefarious Nine

BLACKWATER CANYON RANCH (Western Sexy Romance):
Caleb
Oliver
Justin
Piper
Jesse

ASPEN SERIES (Small Town Sexy Romance):
Wounded (Prequel)
Relentless
Lawless
Cowboys and Angels
Come Back to Me
Surrender
Reckless
Tempted
Crazy One More Time

I'm With You
Breathless

PINECONE VALLEY (Small Town Sexy Romance):
Love Me Again
Love Me Always

RETRIBUTION NOVELS (Sexy Romantic Suspense):
Branded
Hunted
Banished
Hijacked
Betrayed

ARGENT SPRINGS (Small Town Sexy Romance):
Whispers
Secrets

OTHER TITLES:
Moonlight and Margaritas (Sexy Contemporary Romance)
Sweet Vengeance (Sexy Romantic Suspense)

About the Author

Award-winning author Cindy Stark lives with her family and a sweet Border Collie in a small town shadowed by the Rocky Mountains. She writes fun, witch cozy mysteries, emotional romantic suspense, and sexy contemporary romance. She loves to hear from readers!

Connect with her online at:
http://www.CindyStark.com
http://facebook.com/CindyStark19
https://www.goodreads.com/author/show/5895446.Cindy_Stark
https://www.amazon.com/Cindy-Stark/e/B008FT394W

Made in the USA
Monee, IL
14 April 2021